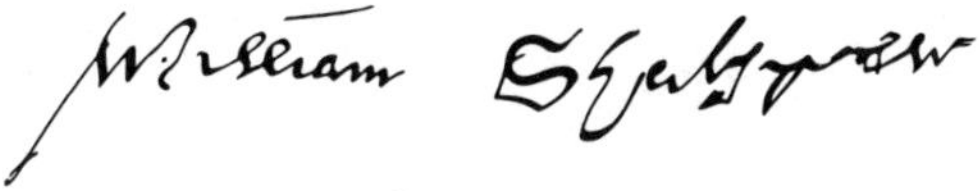

莎士比亚十四行诗

中英双语

SHAKESPEARE'S SONNETS

[英] 威廉·莎士比亚 著 梁实秋 译

湖南文艺出版社
HUNAN LITERATURE AND ART PUBLISHING HOUSE
博集天卷 CS-BOOKY
·长沙·

例 言

一、译文根据莎士比亚原文大部分是“无韵诗”，小部分是散文，更小部分是“押韵的排偶体”。译文一以白话散文为主，但原文中之押韵处以及插曲等则悉译为韵语，以示区别。

二、原文常有版本困难之处，晦涩难解之处亦所在多有，译者酌采一家之说，必要时加以注释。

三、原文多“双关语”，以及各种典故，无法移译时则加注说明。

四、原文多猥亵语，悉照译，以存其真。

目录

序

莎士比亚的《十四行诗》是他的作品中最受人注意的一部，学者及批评家对它钻研之细，致力之勤，仅次于《哈姆雷特》一剧。Sir Walter Raleigh在他的《莎士比亚传》里说："在这神秘窟穴的周围有许多足迹，但其中没有一个是方向朝外的。没有人企图解决这个问题而不留下一本书；于是莎士比亚的神龛上密密杂杂地挂满了这些奉献的祭品，全都枯萎尘封了。"（*Shakespeare*，1907，p.86）有关《十四行诗》的著作，年年都有出现，迄今不衰。其中难题所在，由于客观证据之缺乏，不易解决，难得定论。欲欣赏这些十四行诗，则原诗具在，并无须乞援于考证；欲对之多一些了解，则历年来之有关文献仍自有其价值。兹将有关问题择要略加阐说，以为增加了解之一助。

一　版本

一五九九年W. Jaggard刊印了一个八开本的小册子，其同年发行的第二版的标题页是这样的：

The Passionate Pilgrime. By W. Shakespeare. At London. Printed for W. Jaggard，and are to be sold by W. Leake at the Greyhound in Paules Churchyard. 1599.

这小册子包括二十一首诗，其中只有五首确是莎氏作品，但是这不诚实的出版家竟冒用莎士比亚的名字。Folger Library现藏的一本没有标题页，也许是由于莎士比亚的抗议而抽掉的。那五首确属于莎士比亚的诗，有两首是《十四行诗》的第一三八及第一四四首，文字标点略有出入。另外三首是采自《空爱一场》（*Love's Labour's Lost*）的三首十四行诗，文字标点亦略有出入。这集中的前两首十四行诗，因有异文，倒有了研究的价值，请参看译文注一〇六及注一一七。这是莎士比亚的十四行诗之首次刊印，虽然只有两首。

一六〇九年五月二十日书业公会登记簿有这样的一个记载："a booke called Shakespeares Sonnettes"，同年此书出版，是一个四开本，售价五便士，现存于世者共有十三本，其中的四本之标题页如下：

SHAKESPEARES/SONNETS./Neuer before Imprinted./AT LONDON/By G. Eld for T.T. and are/to be solde by William Aspley/1609./

另有七本之标题页略有部分不同字样如下：

by John Wright，dwelling/at Christ Church gate./1609./

还有两本则没有标题页。

这个四开本的出版家T.T.，即是Thomas Thorpe，他既非印刷者，亦非销售者，他把书稿交人印好之后给两家分别销售。

这四开本收十四行诗一百五十四首，是我们所能看到的唯一的完整本，排印错误之处甚多。据统计，《维诺斯与阿都尼斯》有一千一百九十四行，只有三处轻微错误，而《十四行诗》有二千一百五十五行，错误至少在三打以上，平均每六十行有一错误，标点不在内。卷首献词由T.T.署名，莎士比亚并未出面，而且献词之内文义暧昧，引起后来无穷的揣测（参看下文及注一）。凡此迹象皆足令人疑心此四开本之出版盖未经莎士比亚之授权许可，至少是未经他的校阅。集中第九十九首，有十五行；第一百二十六首只有十二行；第一百四十五首，每行八音节；最后第一百五十三及一百五十四首是翻译性质；而且全集各诗次序有些地方也显得凌乱。这些异常的现象又令人疑心这一诗集的编辑也非出自莎士比亚之手。

四开本虽然舛误甚多，热心拥护的亦不乏人，例如：

George Wyndham：*The Poems of Shakespeare*，1898.

Percy Simpson：*Shakespearean Punctuation*，1911.

但是近代多数批评家都以为四开本不完全可靠，不过最低限度，如威尔孙教授之所主张，我们应该承认四开本所根据的是和莎士比亚原稿相当接近的一种抄本。

一六四〇年（实际是一六三九年），《十四行诗》再度出版，这一回发行人是班孙（John Benson），他是伦敦的一个书商，死于一六六七年，这一本书的名字不是《十四行诗》，而是《诗集》，其标题页如下：

POEMS：/WRITTEN/BY/WIL. SHAKESPEARE./Gent./Printed at *London* by *Tho. Cotes*，and are/to be sold by *John Benson*, dwelling in/*St. Dunstans* Church-yard.1640.

班孙这本书是盗印性质，其内容包括四开本之一百四十六首《十四行诗》（删去的是第十八、十九、四十三、五十六、七十五、七十六诸首，另外两首即第一三八与一四四首则已包括在全部照收的一六一二年版的*The Passionate Pilgrim*之内），此外还有 A *Lover's Complaint*、*The Phoenix and Turtledove*等诗，以及其他诗人的作品如Jonson、Beaumont、Herrick，体裁非常杂乱。他处理这一百四十六首十四行诗的方法也很特殊。他把诗的次序变更了，分别缀成为七十二首，各冠以标题。有些男性的代名词与形容词一律改为女性的，he、his改为she、her，使诗人在诗中致辞的对象一律成为女性。T.T.的献词也删去了。班孙改正了四开本的错误约二十处，但是他增加了新的错误五十处。

班孙的本子在此后一百五十年中发生很大的影响力。第一个十八世纪的编本是Charles Gildon的，刊于一七一〇年，他根据班孙而加以现代化，四年后重刊时成为Nicholas Rowe 的《莎氏戏剧全集》（共六卷）的第七卷。Alexander Pope编的《莎士比亚全集》的第七卷所包括的十四行诗是Dr. George Sewell的编本（一七二五年），也是遵守班孙的传统。此后诸家编本，如Ewing（一七七一年）、Gentleman（一七七四年）、Evans（一七七五年）、Oulton（一八〇四年）、Durrell（一八一七年至一八一八年），都是维持班孙的传统。早在一七一一年出版家Lintot曾翻印四开本（编者姓名不详），但标题页上说："One Hundred and Fifty Four Sonnets, all of them in Praise of his Mistress."，可见亦未脱班孙影响。

一七六六年，Steevens编《莎士比亚戏剧二十种》，附有四开本的十四行诗。Capell曾有一部手稿，修订Lintot印本，未付印，现藏三一学院图书馆，在序中攻击班孙及其附和者。但是真正重振四开本声威的是马龙（Edmond Malone），他有两个编本，第一个刊于一七八〇年，作为Johnson and Steevens合编《莎氏戏剧全集》的补编，第二个刊于一七九〇年，作为他自己编的莎氏全集之第十卷。两个本子都是根据四开本，校勘甚精，且附有评释。

十九世纪早期的版本都是马龙本的翻印，尤其是一七八〇年的那个本子。后来一八三二年Dyce的*Aldine edition*，则倾向于恢复四开本原文，排斥马龙的勘正，这种趋势一直发展下去。十九世纪重要版本有Clark and Aldis Wright编的环球本（一八六四年），第一版剑桥本（一八六六年），第二版剑桥本（一八九三年）。Wyndham的编本前已述及，是绝对拥护四开本的。但是趋于另一极端的是Samuel Butler，他的编本（一八九九年）改动四开本的地方又太多了，常常是不必要的。

二十世纪的编本如Neilson（一九〇六年）、Ridley（一九三四年）、Kittredge（一九三六年）、Harrison（一九三八年）、Bush and Harbage（一九六一年）、Ingram and Redpath（一九六四年）、Wilson（一九六六年）等，有一共同倾向，都是要尽可能保持四开本的面貌。集注本有两种特别值得注意，一个是一九一六年的Alden集注本，另一个是H.E. Rollins新集注本，后者材料特别丰富，一九四四年刊。

二　Mr. W. H. 是谁？

《十四行诗》中的人物有四：（一）诗人自己；（二）诗人的朋友；（三）另一竞争的诗人；（四）黑女人。最重要的是诗人的朋友，因为这些诗大部分（一至一二六）是写给他的。

四开本的献词明白地说Mr. W. H.是“the onlie begetter of these insuing sonnets”，但是何谓“onlie begetter”？onlie = incomparable; peerless（牛津大字典定义五），在此处似不宜作“唯一的”解。更重要的是begetter一字，可以有两种解释：一个是= procurer for another person, obtainer指为发行人搜集十四行诗原稿或抄本的人；一个是inspirer，指引起诗人写作的那个人。二说距离很大。

主前说者可以Sidney Lee为代表（参看他的《莎士比亚传》一九三一年增订版页六八一至六八五）。他认为W.H.是Mr. William Hall，此人乃是伦敦书店学徒出身的一个出版业者，可能是T.T.的一名助理人。William Jaggard于一五九九年刊印了*The Passionate Pilgrim*可能引起了Thomas Thorpe刊印全部莎氏十四行诗的野心，于是W.H.乃大施手腕居然搜求到那一百五十四首诗稿，交给T.T.于一六〇九年印行。这一揣测的主要根据是一六〇六年刊行的一部诗集*A Foure-fould Meditation*，作者为Robert Southwell，这本诗集有由W.H.具名的献词。此一W.H.想来即是《十四行诗》献词中之W.H.。最近A.L. Rowse于一九六三年出版的《莎士比亚传》（页四六三）摭拾旧说以为W.H.是Master William Harvey（即骚赞普顿母亲的第三任丈夫），也是把begetter当作了procurer解。

主后说者意见更分歧，不过最重要的只有两派，一派认为是Henry Wriothesley，the third Earl of Southampton（1573—1624），另一派则认为是William Herbert，the third Earl of Pembroke（1580—1630）。莎士比亚曾把他的两部诗集《维诺斯与阿都尼斯》和《露克利斯的被奸》献给骚赞普顿伯爵。这位伯爵比莎士比亚年轻九岁半，在八岁的时候就袭承了爵位，以后成为文艺的保护人，并且得女王宠，与爱塞克斯昵，两度从征国外。因与爱塞克斯的表妹Elizabeth Vernon先奸后娶，触女王怒，短期下狱，失势甚久。后因牵涉爱塞克斯叛变事败，终身监禁，女王死始得获释。骚赞普顿美丰姿，风流潇洒，与莎士比亚善。Rowe在一七〇九年记载一个故事，据说骚赞普顿有一次曾赠给莎士比亚一千镑钱帮他购置产业。款数甚巨，但非不可能。Nathan Drake于一八一七年在他的*Shakespeare and His Times*一书中之Disquisition on the Object of his Sonnets一篇论文里首先提出W.H.即骚赞普顿的主张。Gerald Massey于一八八八年著*The*

Secret Drama of Shakespeare's Sonnets，继承此说。这两个人主要都是在文字上寻求论证，从客观的莎士比亚交游情形寻求证据最力的当推二十世纪之Mrs. Charlotte Carmichael Stopes，她有两部重要著作：*Shakespeare's Sonnets*（1904）及*The Life of Henry，Third Earl of Southampton, Shakespeare's Patron*（1922）。骚赞普顿一派学说之最大弱点是一五九四年以后他与莎士比亚并无密切友谊的记录，第一对折本的献词没有提到他，十四行诗中也没有提到骚赞普顿后半生之不寻常的遭遇。再则骚赞普顿的名字缩写应是H.W. 而不是W.H. 。

另一派主张W.H.是潘伯娄克伯爵。威廉·赫伯特（William Herbert）生于一五八〇年四月八日，于一六〇一年始承继爵位，早年也是一位风流倜傥的人物。莎士比亚和他的家族渊源甚深。莎氏早年（一五八九至一五九二年间）的戏剧是由名为“潘伯娄克剧团”演出的。此一剧团初现于一五九二年间的记录，旋于一五九三年九月解散。这一群演员的保护人便是这位第三任潘伯娄克伯爵的父亲（他的母亲便是那位著名的潘伯娄克伯爵夫人，其兄Philip Sidney曾为她写了那部著名的*The Countess of Pembroke's Arcadia*）。莎士比亚的第一对折本是献给潘伯娄克兄弟二人的（William Herbert and Philip Herbert），献词中提到潘伯娄克对他的多年知遇。首倡W.H.为潘伯娄克这一学说的是James Boaden（一八三二年），而C.A. Brown: *Shakespeare's Autobiographical Poems*（1838）鼓吹最力。Thomas Tyler（*Shakespeare's Sonnets*，1890）也是最有力的一个支持者。近年的学者们如Hyder Rollins（1944）、J.D. Wilson（1966）、Oscar James Campbell（1964）都倾向于这一派。这一派学说之最大缺点是潘伯娄克于一五九三年时只有十三岁，莎士比亚谆谆劝告这样冲龄的贵族子弟赶快娶妻生子，勿乃不伦？所以潘伯娄克一派总喜欢把《十四行诗》的写作时代稍往后推，同时指陈伊利沙白时代的贵族家庭有提早为子女议婚的习惯。一五九五年，潘伯娄克十五岁，他的父母曾逼他和Elizabeth Carey（即莎氏剧团保护人George Carey，Lord Hunsdon in 1596 and Lord Chamberlain in 1597之女）结婚，订婚初步仪式已经举行，而潘伯娄克仍坚持不允，莎士比亚可能是在这个时候受潘伯娄克的父母之命而撰写那十七首劝告结婚的十四行诗。

此外还有别的学说。例如Richard Farmer（1735—1797）建议说莎士比亚的外甥William Hart

可能即是W.H.，但此说殊不可能，因为他的这个外甥于一六〇〇年方才出世。又如Thomas Tyrwhitt（1730—1797）曾根据第二十首十四行诗之第七行“A man in hew all Hews in his controwling”认为其中有双关义，Hews = Hughes，而第一三五、一三六、一四三所谓Will Sonnets其中又隐含着一个William，从而假想当时有一年轻演员William Hughes，面目姣好，扮演女角，即是诗中之W.H.。此说全无根据，当时各剧团演员名单都还存在，其中没有这个名姓。但是Oscar Wilde于一八八九年写*The Portrait of Mr. W.H.*，仍然根据此一假想敷演成为一篇演义式的论文。最有趣的莫过于D.Barnstorff在一八六〇年所做之建议，以为W.H.即是William Himself之缩写！

无论W.H.是骚赞普顿还是潘伯娄克，献词里何以不直书其名，何以不称其全衔而仅称之为“先生”，我们只能有一个解释，那就是Thorpe没有获得伯爵的同意，以诗的内容而论亦难得当事人的同意，故只好如此地隐约其词了。

三　另一位竞争的诗人是谁？

莎士比亚在他的诗中不断地隐隐约约地提起另一个和他竞争的诗人，此人是谁，引起颇多揣测。较旧的说法是以为此一诗人乃是固定的一个诗人，例如：

Boaden—Daniel（the rival poet）

Cartwright—Marlowe

Bodenstedt—Spenser

Minto—Chapman

Lee—Barnabe Barnes

Henry Brown—Sir John Davies

较新的看法是以为莎士比亚在不同的写作时间所提到的竞争诗人可能不是一个固定的人，而是若干不同的诗人。此一说法似较近情理。

自七十五至八十六诸首，通常认为是有关"竞争的诗人"的部分。实际上第七十六首是意义较为明显的，莎士比亚自承文笔陈腐，比不上时髦作风，他所指的该是John Donne所代表的那一派Metaphysical poetry，而不是固定的哪一个人。不过John Donne确曾一度和潘伯娄克过从甚密。据班章孙说，John Donne的最好作品是二十五岁以前写的，那即是一五九七年以前，而一五九七年正是潘伯娄克庆祝十八岁生日的那一年。莎士比亚所轻视的那种诗，他自己在一六〇一年也试作了一首，那便是*The Phoenix and Turtledove*，也许是他不甘服输，故意在潘伯娄克面前显露一下他的多方面的才华。

第七十八首里所提到的诗人，不是Chapman便是班章孙（参看译本注五十七）。总之是一位学殖较莎士比亚为深的诗人，班章孙的可能性较大。

第七十九、第八十两首，那较大的天才是谁？是马娄还是斯宾塞？

第八十六首像是特指Chapman。他译的荷马史诗《伊利阿德》前七卷刊于一五九八年，用每行十四音节的韵语翻译，确是如莎士比亚在此诗中所说的“声势壮盛”。

四　黑女人是谁？

《十四行诗》自第一至一二六首为一大段，自第一二七至一五二首为另一大段。前一大段是以诗人的朋友为主题，第二大段则以一位黑女人为主题。这黑女人是谁，我们无从确知，但是就诗中所述我们知道她是一个肤色深褐，其貌不扬，但是具有无比的魅力，而且放荡成性，阅人甚多，甚至把莎士比亚的朋友也牵涉在内。像这样的一个女人，在“十四行诗传统”里是没有前例的，显然是实有其人，而且莎士比亚确实与她有不寻常的关系。

如果我们承认W.H.是潘伯娄克，那么顺理成章地我们也应该承认这黑女人大概就是玛丽·菲顿（Mary Fitton）。菲顿是潘伯娄克的情妇。莎士比亚笔下的女人中，罗萨兰（Rosaline）是一个值得注意的角色，例如在《罗密欧与朱丽叶》及《空爱一场》两出戏里的罗萨兰，便都是一个肤色黑的少女。我们有理由相信莎士比亚大概是深深地恋爱过这样的一个黑女人。有许多地方玛丽·菲顿太符合莎士比亚对这黑女人的描述了。

玛丽·菲顿生于一五七八年，于六月二十四日受洗。她的父亲是一位曾在爱尔兰政府服务的Sir Edward Fitton，家住在Gawsworth，Cheshire。她在十七岁时（一五九五年）来到伦敦宫中，翌年奉女王命为宫女（Maid of Honour）。她初到伦敦时就受到潘伯娄克夫人的款待，事实上菲顿先生当年之能晋封爵士便是靠了潘伯娄克夫人（即Mary Sidney）的父亲的力量，所以两家本是早有旧谊的，年轻的威廉·赫伯特很快地就和这位少女发生了情愫。

玛丽·菲顿之所以能顺利地做了宫女，是由于她父亲的老友当时任内廷总管的Sir William Knollys的汲引，他不但照拂她，而且很快地坠入情网，苦追不遂，卒于妻亡之后以六十一的高龄娶了一位十九岁的少女。罗萨兰于《空爱一场》所说“青春的热情燃烧起来没有成年人荒唐得厉害”可能是对他的讽刺（看拙译《空爱一场》第五幕第二景）。

潘伯娄克和玛丽·菲顿的恋情在宫廷里播开了。一六〇一年二月间玛丽怀孕的消息已经不是秘密，潘伯娄克自承与之有染，但是拒绝与之结婚，事闻于女王，女王震怒。三月间玛丽产一男婴，夭折。潘伯娄克下狱，不久开释，玛丽罪罚较轻，只是被逐出宫廷交付看管。除了这一个私生子之外，玛丽还和Sir Richard Leveson私生过两个女儿。玛丽后来又嫁过两个丈夫，一个是Captain Lougher，另一个是Captain Polewhele。

首先提出黑女人即是玛丽·菲顿的是Thomas Tyler，他编的《十四行诗》附有长序说明玛丽的历史，刊于一八九〇年。Frank Harris写《莎士比亚其人》，也接受这一学说。萧伯纳的戏*The Dark Lady of the Sonnets*更给这个故事一个有力的宣传。（较详尽的资料见Lady Newdigate-Newdigate：*Gossip from a Muniment Room; Being passages in the lives of Anne and Mary Fytton*，1907.）

五　著作年代

《十四行诗》不是一个短短时期内写成的。一五九八年秋后Francis Meres: *Palladis Tamia: Wits Treasury*有这样的记述："The sweete wittie soul of Ovid lives in mellifluous and honey-tongued Shakespeare，witnes his Venus and Adonis，his Lucrece，his sugared Sonnets among his private friends，"；随后他又举出莎士比亚为当时若干十四行诗作家之一："most passionate among us to bewaile and bemoane the perplexities of Love."。

这里所谓"甜蜜如糖的十四行诗"，可能只是我们现在所读到的一小部分。

如果我们承认大部分十四行诗是写给潘伯娄克的，那么莎士比亚开始写十四行诗应该是在一五九五年，那年潘伯娄克十五岁，那时候十四行诗正时髦，而且莎士比亚可能是奉潘伯娄克父母之命而写的，已略如前述。四开本的前十七首诗可能即是最早写作的一部分。以后莎士比亚陆续写作，可能一直拖到伊利沙白女王朝代的末尾。

第一百零七首诗是考证写作年代最重要的一首。无疑地里面含有重大的政治事件的影射，但所谓“人间的明月安然度过了她的晦蚀”，意义颇费推敲（看译注七十六）。比较合理的解释大概是指一五九六年伊利沙白女王之渡过了她的六十三岁大关。

六　《十四行诗》的次序

四开本各诗次序可能有若干部分是凌乱的。前十七首自成段落，至一二六为一大段，至一五二为又一大段，这是没有多大问题的，但是如果在诗中寻求一个连贯的故事，则有若干地方不大衔接，可能在一个大段之内或两个大段之间需要加以调整。四开本的次序未必全都正确，班孙的一六四〇年改订本更有问题，所以马龙一七八〇年本又恢复了四开本的次序。近代刊本对于次序之调整各出心裁，由Charles Knight于一八四一年开其端。自班孙以至Tucker

Brooke（1936），据Rollins的记载，有不下二十种不同的调整方法。现在且举一个最近的例，Oscar James Campbell一九六四年编*The Sonnets Songs & Poems of Shakespeare*页二六至二八所提供的意见：

一至十七

诗人致年轻的威廉·赫伯特爵士，后晋袭为潘伯娄克伯爵，二人可能尚未晤面。这一辑诗，通常称为“劝娶妻生子之十四行诗”（procreation sonnets）。

十八至二六

诗人开始攀交。所谓“爱”，即“友谊”之别称；为加强情意，诗人使用性爱之词句。诗人宣称他的作品可以使他的朋友永垂不朽。诗人把这一辑诗连同前一辑诗送呈潘伯娄克，称之为“written ambassage”。

一二七至一三二

按照时间顺序，我们要读诗人致黑女人的最初几首诗。他起初是出之于半戏谑的态度。他赞美她的黑肤色，欣赏她的弹琴。此时必尚未发觉女方对赫伯特的亲昵情形。一度缱绻，又生悔恨。悔恨之余，又极口赞颂其美，唯恐失宠。

二七至四七

诗人外出旅行（二七至三二）。在旅行期间诗人发现其年轻友人与黑女人发生暧昧。诗人责其不义，使之羞惭落泪（三四）。诗人感其知悔，恕之，仍旧和好。至第四十首，友人又与黑女人私通。诗人对此二度犯罪加以曲谅，认定黑女之诱惑难以抵御。在四十二首里诗人坦然承认他与友人乃异体同心，对黑女之双方示爱并无芥蒂。

一三三至一四二

黑女二度不忠之后，诗人分析形势，认为她应负主要责任。一三五至一三七首，即所谓 Will sonnets，诗人直斥之为“大众碇泊的湾港”，因她有人尽可夫之欲望。诗人知其不义，仍不能忘情，衷心苦痛。

四八至六六

诗人焦虑沮丧。朋友不忠及人生无常为主要课题。

六七至一〇八

自剖忏悔之余，诗人又与朋友书翰往来。六七至七十首劝潘伯娄克慎交游。七十五至九十九首诗人忠谏未被采纳，苦恼彷徨。第一百首，心情一变，诗人对朋友之误会顿消，又复沉醉于友情之中。

一四三至一五二

诗人把黑女人形容为一个舍弃婴儿追逐鸡群的主妇，向她求宠。他自知为情所缚无法挣脱。一五二首表示大梦初醒，毅然在心理上表示决绝。

一〇九至一二六

诗人最后向潘伯娄克解释，友谊几被黑女人所离间，友谊仍可恢复，永久不渝。

七　十四行诗的传统与时尚

十四行诗始于何时，已不甚可考。十三世纪时在意大利已经有人写作。最著名的是皮特拉克（Petrarch，1304—1374），他写了一连串的三百一十七首十四行诗歌颂他的可望而不可即的爱人Lady Laura。莎士比亚在《罗密欧与朱丽叶》（第二幕第四景）里提起过皮特拉克及其爱人。自皮特拉克起，十四行诗写作风气盛行，几达三个世纪之久，形成为一种传统。若干首诗一定是同一主题，联成一系，所谓sonnet sequence。诗中的对象是一位风姿绝世的女郎，她不但是一位有血有肉的美人，也代表至高无上的理想美。她冷若冰霜，她高不可攀。诗人既感青睐之难得，又伤流光之易逝，柔肠寸结，缠绵悱恻。此种作风，几成定型，所用文辞亦多夸张之比喻。而对于诗之永久不朽的价值之推崇，亦为习见之事。

十四行诗的风尚由意大利传入法兰西，著名作者包括Ronsard、du Bellay、Desportes。流入英国是从Wyatt and Surrey之翻译皮特拉克开始，他们的翻译收在他们死后才刊行的*Tottel's Miscellany*里面（一五五七年）。十四行诗在英国成为风尚是由于Philip Sidney所作的*Astrophel and Stella*，刊于一五九一年之春。嗣后五年之内陆续刊行的著名的十四行诗集很多，例如：

Daniel：*Delia*，1592

Lodge：*Phyllis*，1593

Constable：*Diana*，1592

Drayton：*Idea*，1594

Spenser：*Amoretti*，1595

莎士比亚的十四行诗大概亦即作于此时。不过在形式上和内容方面，莎士比亚的十四行诗和皮特拉克的传统都有出入。皮特拉克的十四行诗，分前后两段，前段八行，所谓octave，其脚韵的排列为abbaabba；后段六行，所谓sestet，可以有两个或三个脚韵，排列次序不止一种，不过末两行必不押韵。全诗主意在前段中完全写尽，后段仅是评述阐释以为结束。莎士比亚的诗则形式略异，诗十四行，每行十音节，抑扬格，分三个quatrain，各四行，最后两行，其脚韵的排列为abab，cdcdefef，gg。（但亦有几个例外，第九九首为十五行，第一二六首为十二行英雄诗体，第一四八首每行八音节）。莎士比亚的这种诗体不是他的创造，在一五七五年Gascoigne在他的*Certayne Notes of Instruction*里已经为英国式的十四行诗体加以明白的描述了:

“Some thinke that all Poems（being short）may be called Sonets，as in deede it is a diminutive word derived of Sonare，but yet can best allowe to call those Sonets whiche are of fourteene lynes，every line conteyning tenne syllables. The first twelve do ryme in staves of foure lines by crosse meetre，and the last two ryming togither do conclude the whole.”

在莎士比亚手里，此种形式使用到了最纯熟的地步，故我们称之为“莎士比亚体之十四行诗”，而不称之为“Surrey体”。不过莎士比亚偶然也在第八行与第九行之间做一截断，与意大利体无异，如第二九、二一至二三、七一、七二、七六各首。在内容上则莎士比亚的诗不合于传统之处亦甚明显。例如诗中主题并不以爱情为限，而且诗中的女主人并不拒人千里之外，诗人也未表达一般失恋的人所有的苦楚。最值得注意的是大部分诗是写给一位男士的。显然地，莎士比亚在沿袭十四行诗传统之余，也还抒写了他个人当时的各种感触，描述了他个人当时的各种经验。

给男朋友写情诗，在当时也许不是太稀奇的事。文艺复兴期间的人非常重视友谊。《圣经》上早就宣示David and Jonathan的友好之情“超过了对女人的爱”。一五七一年Richard Edwards的*Damon and Pythias*，一五七九年John Lyly的*Euphues or the Anatomy of Wit*，都是对友谊大加赞扬。Lyly说过这样的话：

The love of men and women is a thing common and of course：the friendship of man is infinite and immortal. Love is but an eye-worm，which only tickleth the head with hopes and wishes；friendship the image of eternity，in which there is nothing moveable，nothing mischievous....Friendship standeth stiffly in storms. Time draweth wrinkles in a fair face，but addeth fresh colours to a fast friend，which neither heat，nor cold，nor place，nor destiny can alter or diminish.

大意是说："男女之爱乃事所当然，男人之友谊乃无限而神圣的。爱情不过是眼皮底下的一条丝虫，刺激头部，使生欲望；友谊则是永恒的象征，其中没有游移没有虚诈……于惊涛骇浪之中友谊屹立不动。时间给姣好的面貌上刻画皱纹，但是给忠贞的朋友增加鲜艳的色彩，真实的朋友不是人间冷暖、地位、命运所能改变或削弱的。"莎士比亚诗中对男友所表示的爱，是友谊的爱。

这样的解释似仍嫌不足，因为莎士比亚在诗里屡屡明显地表示他爱他的男友乃是爱他的美貌。直到十七世纪Sir Thomas Browne在他的*Religio Medici*里还称颂友谊之可贵远在对父母、妻子的情感之上，仅次于对上帝之爱。但莎士比亚在诗里没有表现出多少宗教色彩，他的爱就是人性的爱（虽然也有人过分地重视了第一四六首字面的意义）。我们与其强调友谊爱之理想境界，不如面对现实地承认一个男人可能对一个年轻的面目俊俏的男人发生一种不寻常的爱。Sidney是著名的十四行诗作家，他爱的是一位求之未得的少女，亦即诗中之Stella，但是他也有一段不甚寻常的友谊经验。他十八岁时遨游欧陆，在德国遇到一位五十四岁的Herbert Languet，顿成莫逆。Languet爱的是他的风度翩翩，翰札往来，情致缠绵。可见这种不寻常的忘年交在事实上是可能的。不过同性间的爱也有不同的表达方式，我们在莎士比亚写给潘伯娄克的那些首诗里，找不到任何证据足以指控他犯有实际同性爱的罪行。第二十首是常为人诟病的，George Steevens在一七八〇年就说：“读到这一首写给一个男人的言不由衷的赞颂词，便不能不有厌恶与愤慨交加之感。”（“impossible to read this fulsome panegyrick，addressed to a male object，without an equal admixture of disgust and indignation.”）其实这一首诗正好可以说明莎士比亚对他的朋友的关系只是精神的爱，断袖癖的罪名是加不上去的。关于此点，Edward Hubler教授有很透彻的解释，他说：“关于莎士比亚的性生活，无可争辩的证据是这样的，十八岁时他娶了一位比他大八岁的女人。结婚六个月后他做了父亲。一年又九个月后他再度做了父亲，这一回生的是孪生儿。很明显地，他早年的性生活完全是异性的，没有任何证据说他是同性恋者，当然也没有证据说他不是。一个男人若不打老婆，他的克制功夫是不会有记载的。双方面皆无绝对证据。我们只好推测其可能性，一个人在青年从事异性恋的人以后大概不至于深陷于同性恋事件之中。这种事当然也曾经有过，不过以统计的观点来说，发生的可能性不大。对莎士比亚可能没有发生过。”（*The Sense of Shakespeare's Sonnets*，1952，页一五五）。

华滋渥斯（Wordsworth）的著名诗句：

“勿轻视十四行诗；批评家，你皱眉，
忘了它的光荣历史；用这钥匙
莎士比亚打开了他的心。”

（Scorn not the sonnet；Critic，you have frowned，Mindless of its just honour；with this key Shakespeare unlocked his heart.）

莎士比亚真的把他的心事都在诗中倾诉出来了吗？Sidney Lee本来是这样相信的，后来又改变了意见，以为莎士比亚的诗只是传统的模拟之作。平心而论，这些十四行诗不可能没有自传的成分，但是我们难以确定其中的事迹罢了。抒情诗与戏剧不同，不可能全是无病呻吟，更不可能是借题发挥。诗的文字有时是不免于夸张，有时不免于隐晦，诗里面的思想与情感却是真的。后人连篇累牍地考证文字，本身是有趣的，但足以转移读者对诗的本身之注意。Rollins教授说得好：“如果Thorpe没有写那三十个字，如今无疑地会有更多的人把这些十四行诗当作诗来读！”

TO.THE.ONLIE.BEGETTER.OF.
THESE.INSUING.SONNETS.
Mr.W.H. ALL.HAPPINESSE.
AND.THAT.ETERNITIE.
PROMISED.
BY.
OUR.EVER–LIVING.POET.
WISHETH.
THE.WELL–WISHING.
ADVENTURER.IN.
SETTING.
FORTH.
T. T.

献 词[1]

发行人于发刊之际敬谨祝贺
下列十四行诗之无比的主人翁
W.H. 先生幸福无量并克享
不朽诗人所许下之千古盛名
T.T.

Sonnet 1

From fairest creatures we desire increase,
That thereby beauty's rose might never die,
But as the riper should by time decease,
His tender heir might bear his memory:
But thou, contracted to thine own bright eyes,
Feed'st thy light's flame with self–substantial fuel,
Making a famine where abundance lies,
Thyself thy foe, to thy sweet self too cruel.
Thou that art now the world's fresh ornament,
And only herald to the gaudy spring,
Within thine own bud buriest thy content,
And, tender churl, mak'st waste in niggarding:
  Pity the world, or else this glutton be,
  To eat the world's due, by the grave and thee.

[2]

愿最美的人能多多生育，

使青春美貌的花朵永久不朽，

成熟的到时候总要死去，

他的幼嗣可以继续他的风流。

但是你，只看中你自己的亮眼睛，

用自身做燃料培养那眼里的火焰，

在丰收之际造成了饥馑的灾情。

与自己为敌，对自己未免过于凶残。

你是当今世界之鲜艳的装饰品，

是烂漫春光之无比的一朵奇葩，

你竟在自己的蓓蕾里埋葬你的子孙。

吝啬鬼，你越是舍不得你是越糟蹋。

　　怜悯这世界吧，否则你便是个饕餮的人，

　　你独身而死，你吞食了这世界应得的一份。

Sonnet 2

When forty winters shall besiege thy brow,
And dig deep trenches in thy beauty's field,
Thy youth's proud livery so gazed on now
Will be a tottered weed of small worth held:
Then being asked, where all thy beauty lies,
Where all the treasure of thy lusty days,
To say within thine own deep–sunken eyes
Were an all–eating shame, and thriftless praise.
How much more praise deserved thy beauty's use,
If thou couldst answer, 'This fair child of mine
Shall sum my count, and make my old excuse',
Proving his beauty by succession thine.
    This were to be new made when thou art old,
    And see thy blood warm when thou feel'st it cold.

二

四十个冬天围攻你的容颜[3]，
在你美貌平原上挖掘壕沟的时候，
你的青春盛装，如今被人艳羡，
将变成不值一顾的褴褛破旧。
那时有人要问，你的美貌现在何地，
你青春时代的宝藏都在什么地方。
你若回答说，在你深陷的眼坑里，
那将是自承贪婪，对浪费的赞扬[4]。
拿你的美貌去投资生息岂不更好！
你可这样回答："我这孩子多么漂亮，
他将为我结账，弥补我的衰老。"
他的美貌和你的是一模一样！
　　这就好像你衰老之后又重新翻造一遍，
　　你觉得血已冰冷又再度觉得温暖。

Sonnet 3

Look in thy glass and tell the face thou viewest,
Now is the time that face should form another,
Whose fresh repair if now thou not renewest,
Thou dost beguile the world, unbless some mother.
For where is she so fair whose uneared womb
Disdains the tillage of thy husbandry?
Or who is he so fond will be the tomb
Of his self–love to stop posterity?
Thou art thy mother's glass, and she in thee
Calls back the lovely April of her prime;
So thou through windows of thine age shalt see,
Despite of wrinkles, this thy golden time.
But if thou live remember'd not to be,
Die single, and thine image dies with thee.

三

照照镜子，告诉你看到的那张脸
现在时间已到，该把那脸另换一张。
如果现在你不重整你的焕发的容颜，
你辜负世人，使一个做母亲的失望。
哪个女人那样美，她那未开垦的子宫
会拒绝你去耕耘？
哪个男人那样蠢，顾影自怜地把命断送，
而心甘情愿地断子绝孙？
你是你母亲的镜子，她看到你
便忆起她的青春愉快的时光。
你将来皱纹满面，从你老年窗扉望出去，
同样也可窥见你黄金时代的景象。
　　但是你若虚度一生，只愿死后被人忘记，
　　那么就独身一世，你和你的踪影一同死去。

Sonnet 4

Unthrifty loveliness, why dost thou spend
Upon thyself thy beauty's legacy?
Nature's bequest gives nothing, but doth lend,
And being frank she lends to those are free:
Then, beauteous niggard, why dost thou abuse
The bounteous largess given thee to give?
Profitless usurer, why dost thou use
So great a sum of sums, yet canst not live?
For having traffic with thyself alone,
Thou of thyself thy sweet self dost deceive:
Then how when Nature calls thee to be gone,
What àcceptable audit canst thou leave?
    Thy unused beauty must be tombed with thee,
    Which usèd lives th'executor to be.

四

不事积蓄的人儿，你的美貌的产业
为什么都在你自己身上挥霍净尽?
造物主不做任何赠予，只是暂借，
她本身豪爽，只肯借给慷慨的人们。
美貌的吝啬鬼，你为什么滥用了
那份给了你要你再给人的丰富资产?
不善经营资产的人，你何以花掉
这样多的资产而还不能活得久远?
因为你只是和自己交易往来[5]，
你甘心欺骗你的可爱的自己。
等造物主有一天叫你走开，
你留下的账目如何交代下去?
　　你未加运用的美貌将随你一同入殓，
　　若善为利用，会做你的遗产执行人。

Sonnet 5

Those hours that with gentle work did frame
The lovely gaze where every eye doth dwell
Will play the tyrants to the very same,
And that unfair which fairly doth excel;
For never–resting time leads summer on
To hideous winter and confounds him there,
Sap checked with frost and lusty leaves quite gone,
Beauty o'ersnowed and bareness every where:
Then were not summer's distillation left
A liquid prisoner pent in walls of glass,
Beauty's effect with beauty were bereft,
Nor it nor no remembrance what it was.
    But flowers distilled, though they with winter meet,
    Leese but their show; their substance still lives sweet.

五

时间，以巧妙的手艺创造
那众人瞩目的可爱的容颜，
有一日要对它变得非常粗暴，
把那绝世之姿变成丑陋不堪。
永无休止的时间引导着夏季
到可怕的冬天，就在那里把它毁伤：
浆液被寒霜凝结，绿叶全无踪迹，
美貌覆上了冰雪，到处一片凄凉。
如在夏季不曾提炼香花的精华，
把那香水密封在玻璃瓶里，
美的芬芳和美的本身将一起被糟蹋。
本身无存，也没有什么可供回忆。
　　花儿一经提炼，纵然遇到冬天，
　　只是花颜失色，其芬芳永在人间。

Sonnet 6

Then let not winter's ragged hand deface
In thee thy summer ere thou be distilled:
Make sweet some vial; treasure thou some place
With beauty's treasure ere it be self–killed:
That use is not forbidden usury
Which happies those that pay the willing loan;
That's for thyself to breed another thee,
Or ten times happier be it ten for one;
Ten times thyself were happier than thou art,
If ten of thine ten times refigured thee:
Then what could death do if thou shouldst depart,
Leaving thee living in posterity?
    Be not self–willed, for thou art much too fair
    To be death's conquest and make worms thine heir.

六

那么在你的精华未加提炼以前，
不要让严冬的粗手把你的盛夏毁伤。
把香水装进一个瓶里，趁它尚未消散，
把这宝藏放进一个宝贵的地方。
那不算是违法的高利贷，
若能使举债付息的人们得到幸福。
那乃是你自己又滋生一个你出来，
若是生出十个便是十倍的满足[6]。
十倍的你将比你现在十倍的快乐。
如果十个孩子都长得完全像你，
你逝世的时候死神能奈你何，
看着你在后代中安然生活下去？
　　不要任性，因为你这样的美于姿容，
　　不可被死神强占[7]，不可让蛆虫继承。

Sonnet 7

Lo in the orient when the gracious light
Lifts up his burning head, each under eye
Doth homage to his new–appearing sight,
Serving with looks his sacred majesty;
And having climbed the steep–up heavenly hill,
Resembling strong youth in his middle age,
Yet mortal looks adore his beauty still,
Attending on his golden pilgrimage:
But when from highmost pitch, with weary car,
Like feeble age he reeleth from the day,
The eyes (fore duteous) now converted are
From his low tract and look another way:
So thou, thyself outgoing in thy noon,
Unlooked on diest unless thou get a son.

七

看，那慈祥的光明从东方
抬起了他的火红的头，下界众生
都膜拜他这新出现的景象，
以恭顺的眼光注视着他的威风；
他爬上了半空中陡峻的山，
像是一个踏入中年的壮丁，
人们仍然仰慕他的美丽容颜，
注视着他的辉煌的旅程；
但是从那最高顶点，驾着疲惫的车辆，
像一个衰弱老者，他蹒跚地从白昼踱出，
以前恭顺的眼睛现在转了方向，
不再注视他的下坡的路途：
　　你也是一样，你自己的正午转眼即逝[8]，
　　死也无人管，除非你能生个儿子。

Sonnet 8

Music to hear, why hear'st thou music sadly?
Sweets with sweets war not, joy delights in joy:
Why lov'st thou that which thou receiv'st not gladly,
Or else receiv'st with pleasure thine annoy?
If the true concord of well–tunèd sounds,
By unions married, do offend thine ear,
They do but sweetly chide thee, who confounds
In singleness the parts that thou shouldst bear;
Mark how one string, sweet husband to another,
Strikes each in each by mutual ordering;
Resembling sire, and child, and happy mother,
Who all in one, one pleasing note do sing;
  Whose speechless song being many, seeming one,
  Sings this to thee, 'Thou single wilt prove none.'

八[9]

你的声音如音乐，你听音乐何以要凄怆？
甜的与甜的不相冲突，快乐的喜欢快乐的事物。
不能愉快接受的东西，你何以还要受赏？
难道你是高高兴兴地接受这份悲苦？
如果真正和谐的音调
配合无间，使你听着不舒服，
那便是它在曼声地谴责你，你破坏了
生命的和谐而宁愿孤独。
听，一根弦像是另一根的亲爱夫妻，
彼此交响起来，是多么地琴瑟调和；
像是父、子和快乐母亲的关系，
齐声唱出一支悦耳的歌：
　　这无词的歌，像是一声出自众口，
　　对你歌唱：“你独身则将一无所有。”

Sonnet 9

Is it for fear to wet a widow's eye
That thou consum'st thyself in single life?
Ah! if thou issueless shalt hap to die,
The world will wail thee like a makeless wife;
The world will be thy widow and still weep,
That thou no form of thee hast left behind,
When every private widow well may keep,
By children's eyes, her husband's shape in mind:
Look what an unthrift in the world doth spend
Shifts but his place, for still the world enjoys it,
But beauty's waste hath in the world an end,
And kept unused the user so destroys it:
    No love toward others in that bosom sits
    That on himself such murd'rous shame commits.

九

你是否怕湿了一个寡妇的眼睛，
所以独身不娶，糟蹋你自己？
啊！如果你死后没有人继承，
世人都会像寡妇一般地哭你；
世人都将是你的遗孀，长久地哀悼，
怨你没有留下你的形影，
而真正的寡妇却能回忆丈夫的容貌，
只消看看孩子们的眼睛。
看，一个浪子在世间挥霍金钱，
金钱只是换了主，依然由人享用；
但是美貌一糟蹋就算完，
留着不用便是自己把它断送。
　　一个人这样凶狠把自己毁坏，
　　心中不会对别人有半点慈爱。

Sonnet 10

For shame deny that thou bear'st love to any,
Who for thyself art so unprovident.
Grant, if thou wilt, thou art beloved of many,
But that thou none lov'st is most evident;
For thou art so possessed with murd'rous hate,
That 'gainst thyself thou stick'st not to conspire,
Seeking that beauteous roof to ruinate
Which to repair should be thy chief desire:
O change thy thought, that I may change my mind!
Shall hate be fairer lodged than gentle love?
Be as thy presence is, gracious and kind,
Or to thyself at least kind–hearted prove:
    Make thee another self for love of me,
    That beauty still may live in thine or thee.

一〇

说什么你对任何人怀有爱意[10]，
你对你自己如此地漠不关心！
你要承认，是有许多人爱你，
很显然地，你并不爱任何人。
因为你的嫉恨实在是太凶恶，
甚至对你自己都存心不良，
一心想要毁灭那美丽的躯壳，
其实你该对它如意地装潢。
改变你的主张吧，我好改变我的观感！
恨的住处难道比爱的更为漂亮？
要像你的外表一般，温柔而和善，
至少要对你自己有慈爱的心肠。
　　为了爱我起见，请再造出一个你来，
　　让美貌在你或你的孩子身上永久存在。

Sonnet 11

As fast as thou shalt wane, so fast thou grow'st
In one of thine, from that which thou departest,
And that fresh blood which youngly thou bestow'st
Thou mayst call thine, when thou from youth convertest:
Herein lives wisdom, beauty, and increase,
Without this, folly, age, and cold decay:
If all were minded so, the times should cease,
And threescore year would make the world away.
Let those whom Nature hath not made for store,
Harsh, featureless, and rude, barrenly perish:
Look whom she best endowed she gave the more;
Which bounteous gift thou shouldst in bounty cherish:
  She carved thee for her seal, and meant thereby,
  Thou shouldst print more, not let that copy die.

十一

你衰歇得快，但是在你滋生出来的[11]
儿子身上你也生长得一样迅速；
你青春时候投注下的新鲜血液，
到你衰老时，便有了你原来的面目。
这样做便有智慧、美貌和滋生，
否则便只有愚蠢、老迈和腐朽。
如果大家与你做同样想，人类将要绝种，
六十年的时间将使世界一无所有。
有些人造物主本无意把他们繁殖起来——
粗制滥造——无妨让他们断子绝孙，
但你是灵秀所钟得天独厚的人才[12]，
便该把这一份丰盛的秉赋永久保存。
　　造物主把你雕刻成为她的印玺，
　　为的是要你多多盖印，不可予以废弃[13]。

Sonnet 12

When I do count the clock that tells the time,
And see the brave day sunk in hideous night,
When I behold the violet past prime,
And sable curls all silvered o'er with white,
When lofty trees I see barren of leaves,
Which erst from heat did canopy the herd,
And summer's green all girded up in sheaves
Borne on the bier with white and bristly beard:
Then of thy beauty do I question make
That thou among the wastes of time must go,
Since sweets and beauties do themselves forsake,
And die as fast as they see others grow,
    And nothing 'gainst Time's scythe can make defence
    Save breed to brave him when he takes thee hence.

一二

我数着报时的钟声，

看着大好的白昼陷入夜晚；

我看到紫罗兰开过了全盛，

一层银白罩上了貂黑的发鬈；

我看见曾为牧群遮阴的高树，

如今树叶已经完全脱光，

夏季的绿苗都紧紧捆扎成束，

带着白硬芒须被抬了去埋葬。

于是对于你的美貌我就开始担心，

恐怕你要随着时间而被淘汰，

因为美妙的事物总要蠲弃自身，

很快地死去，看着别个生长起来。

　　时间的镰刀没人能够阻挡，

　　除非是你被抓走，让孩子去抵抗。

Sonnet 13

O that you were your self! but, love, you are
No longer yours than you yourself here live;
Against this coming end you should prepare,
And your sweet semblance to some other give:
So should that beauty which you hold in lease
Find no determination; then you were
Your self again after yourself's decease,
When your sweet issue your sweet form should bear.
Who lets so fair a house fall to decay,
Which husbandry in honour might uphold
Against the stormy gusts of winter's day
And barren rage of death's eternal cold?
　O none but unthrifts: dear my love, you know
　You had a father, let your son say so.

一三

愿你能永久不变！但是，爱人，
你逃不过你的尘世间的寿命，
你要准备这个末日的来临。
把你的美貌让另外一个人继承，
那么你所租赁的美丽形体
将永无尽期。在你死后
你将再度是你自己，
你的美丽形体由你的美丽子孙保有。
有这样漂亮的房子，谁肯任其坍倒，
如果善为安排即可抗拒
冬季的风狂雨暴
和冷酷的死神之无情的打击？
　　啊，除了败家子谁也不肯：我的朋友，你晓得，
　　你曾有过父亲，让你的儿子也能这样说。

Sonnet 14

Not from the stars do I my judgement pluck,
And yet methinks I have astronomy,
But not to tell of good or evil luck,
Of plagues, of dearths, or seasons' quality;
Nor can I fortune to brief minutes tell,
Pointing to each his thunder, rain, and wind,
Or say with princes if it shall go well
By oft predict that I in heaven find:
But from thine eyes my knowledge I derive,
And, constant stars, in them I read such art
As truth and beauty shall together thrive
If from thy self to store thou wouldst convert:
    Or else of thee this I prognosticate,
    Thy end is truth's and beauty's doom and date.

一四

我的判断不是靠了星象而来，
但是星象学我想我也懂一点，
不过我不会预言运气的好坏，
疫疠，灾荒，或四季的吉凶变迁；
我也不能为人卜算流年，
指点出某时某刻有迅雷风雨；
我也不能靠什么朕兆出现在天边，
就对帝王们预报什么灾异。
但是从你的眼睛我获得了学问，
从你的两颗星眸我得到这样的指点：
“真与美将同时并存，
如果你肯把你自己传诸久远。”
　　否则我可以对你预告：
　　“你死之日便是真与美的末日来到。”

Sonnet 15

When I consider every thing that grows
Holds in perfection but a little moment,
That this huge stage presenteth nought but shows
Whereon the stars in secret influence comment;
When I perceive that men as plants increase,
Cheerèd and checked even by the selfsame sky,
Vaunt in their youthful sap, at height decrease,
And wear their brave state out of memory:
Then the conceit of this inconstant stay
Sets you most rich in youth before my sight,
Where wasteful Time debateth with Decay
To change your day of youth to sullied night,
　　And all in war with Time for love of you,
　　As he takes from you, I ingraft you new.

一五

我有时思量，生长的百物
其全盛时期都非常地短暂，
人生舞台只有戏剧的演出，
由满天星斗暗中指导评判；
我有时看出，人和草木一样生长，
受同一老天的鼓舞与训斥，
在青春时候趾高气扬，
盛极而衰，盛况从记忆中消逝。
所以，想到了人生无常，
我愈发觉得你年少翩翩，
这时节光阴正在和毁灭商量，
要把你的灿烂青春变为黑暗的夜晚。
　　我为了爱你而与光阴奋斗，
　　我要为你移植新枝[14]，他要把你的生命夺走。

Sonnet 16

But wherefore do not you a mightier way
Make war upon this bloody tyrant Time,
And fortify yourself in your decay
With means more blessèd than my barren rhyme?
Now stand you on the top of happy hours,
And many maiden gardens, yet unset,
With virtuous wish would bear your living flowers,
Much liker than your painted counterfeit:
So should the lines of life that life repair
Which this time's pencil or my pupil pen
Neither in inward worth nor outward fair
Can make you live yourself in eyes of men:
  To give away yourself keeps yourself still,
  And you must live drawn by your own sweet skill.

一六

但你为何不对这凶恶的暴君，时间，
以更强硬的方式去作战？
你为何不采取比我这无力的诗篇
更为有效的自卫的手段？
你如今正在幸运的巅峰状态，
许多尚未播种的处女园地，
都愿为你开出活的花儿来，
比你的画像要更为像你。
所以，寿命应该由儿女加以伸展，
世间的画家或我这支拙笔，
无论怎样描绘你内心的秀美或外在的容颜，
都无法使你长久存在人们的眼里。
　　牺牲自我便可保存自我于永久[15]，
　　用你自己的妙笔去画，即可长生不朽。

Sonnet 17

Who will believe my verse in time to come
If it were filled with your most high deserts?
Though yet, heaven knows, it is but as a tomb
Which hides your life, and shows not half your parts.
If I could write the beauty of your eyes,
And in fresh numbers number all your graces,
The age to come would say, 'This poet lies;
Such heavenly touches ne'er touched earthly faces.'
So should my papers (yellowed with their age)
Be scorned, like old men of less truth than tongue,
And your true rights be termed a poet's rage
And stretchèd metre of an àntique song:
    But were some child of yours alive that time,
    You should live twice, in it and in my rhyme.

一七

后世谁会相信我的诗篇，

如果里面都是对你绝口称赞？

虽然，天晓得，我的诗像坟一般

遮盖了你的生命，没能表扬你的才华一半。

如果我能写出你的眼睛的漂亮，

以清新的诗句记述你的仪态，

后世一定要说：“这诗人说谎，

如此神妙之笔不曾触到凡人脸上来。”

于是我的诗稿，旧得发黄，

被人轻蔑，好像是信口胡说的老人，

把你本来面目看成为诗人的狂想，

一首古代诗歌之夸张的翻新。

　　但是那时节如果你有子孙，

　　靠子孙，靠我的诗，你将双倍地永存。

Sonnet 18

Shall I compare thee to a summer's day?
Thou art more lovely and more temperate:
Rough winds do shake the darling buds of May,
And summer's lease hath all too short a date;
Sometime too hot the eye of heaven shines,
And often is his gold complexion dimmed;
And every fair from fair sometime declines,
By chance or nature's changing course untrimmed:
But thy eternal summer shall not fade,
Nor lose possession of that fair thou ow'st,
Nor shall Death brag thou wand'rest in his shade,
When in eternal lines to time thou grow'st.
    So long as men can breathe or eyes can see,
    So long lives this, and this gives life to thee.

一八 [16]

我可能把你和夏天相比拟？

你比夏天更可爱更温和。

狂风会把五月的花苞吹落地[17]，

夏天也嫌太短促，匆匆而过；

有时太阳照得太热，

常常又遮暗他的金色的脸。

美的事物总不免要凋落，

偶然的，或是随自然变化而流转。

但是你的永恒之夏不会褪色，

你不会失去你的俊美的仪容。

死神不能夸说你在他的阴影里面走着，

如果你在这不朽的诗句里获得了永生。

　　只要人们能呼吸，眼睛能看东西，

　　此诗就会不朽，使你永久生存下去。

Sonnet 19

Devouring Time, blunt thou the lion's paws,
And make the earth devour her own sweet brood;
Pluck the keen teeth from the fierce tiger's jaws,
And burn the long-lived phoenix in her blood;
Make glad and sorry seasons as thou fleet'st,
And do whate'er thou wilt, swift-footed Time,
To the wide world and all her fading sweets;
But I forbid thee one most heinous crime:
O carve not with thy hours my love's fair brow,
Nor draw no lines there with thine àntique pen;
Him in thy course untainted do allow
For beauty's pattern to succeeding men.
    Yet do thy worst, old Time: despite thy wrong,
    My love shall in my verse ever live young.

一九

吞噬一切的时间哪，你磨钝狮子的爪，
你使尘世吞食她自己的亲生孩子；
从猛虎嘴里把锐利的牙齿拔掉，
把长命的凤凰活生生地自行烧死；
你一面飞驰，一面造成多少欢欣悲戚。
捷足的时间哟，这广大的世界
及一切美好脆弱的东西由你随便处理，
但我不准你做一桩最可恶的祸害：
别在我的爱友的额上镌刻横纹，
也别用你的笔在脸上胡乱画线；
你在途中不要让他受到伤损，
好给后世的男人留一个美貌的模范。
　　不过你尽管发威，时间。不怕你为害，
　　我的好友在我的诗里将青春永在。

Sonnet 20

A woman's face with Nature's own hand painted
Hast thou, the master–mistress of my passion;
A woman's gentle heart, but not acquainted
With shifting change, as is false women's fashion;
An eye more bright than theirs, less false in rolling,
Gilding the object whereupon it gazeth;
A man in hue, all hues in his controlling,
Which steals men's eyes and women's souls amazeth.
And for a woman wert thou first created,
Till Nature as she wrought thee fell a–doting,
And by addition me of thee defeated,
By adding one thing to my purpose nothing.
  But since she pricked thee out for women's pleasure,
  Mine be thy love, and thy love's use their treasure.

二〇[18]

你有一张女人的脸，
是造物亲笔画的，是我诗中热情之所寄；
你有一颗女人的温柔的心，但并未沾染
一般轻浮女子之善变的恶习。
你的眼比她们的亮，不那样虚伪地流盼，
你看到什么便给什么镀上了金；
你风度翩翩，压倒了一切美貌少年，
使男人们目眩，使女人们倾心。
造物主原想把你造成一位女郎，
后来在造你的时候爱上了你，
为了使我对你大为失望，
在你身上添了一件对我无用的东西。
　　她既然选中了你，要你讨女人的欢心，
　　把你的爱给我，把情欲送给她们。

Sonnet 21

So is it not with me as with that Muse,
Stirred by a painted beauty to his verse,
Who heaven itself for ornament doth use,
And every fair with his fair doth rehearse,
Making a couplement of proud compare
With sun and moon, with earth and sea's rich gems,
With April's first–born flowers, and all things rare
That heaven's air in this huge rondure hems.
O let me, true in love, but truly write,
And then believe me, my love is as fair
As any mother's child, though not so bright
As those gold candles fixed in heaven's air:
    Let them say more that like of hearsay well,
    I will not praise that purpose not to sell.

二一

我和那诗人可大不相同。
他见了打扮漂亮的女人就勾起诗意，
不惜使用天堂来肆意形容，
用各种美丽的东西和他的美人相比。
竟敢这样大言不惭地比拟，
说他的美人媲美日、月、水陆的奇珍，
四月初放的鲜花，以及天空大气
圈在这世上的一切稀罕的物品。
我是真心相爱，只能说老实话，
请相信我，我的爱人的容颜
和任何女人生的人不相上下，
虽然不及镶在天空的金烛那么灿烂。
　　爱说陈词滥调的人们让他们说去，
　　我无须夸赞，因为我无意出售你。

Sonnet 22

My glass shall not persuade me I am old,
So long as youth and thou are of one date,
But when in thee time's furrows I behold,
Then look I death my days should expiate:
For all that beauty that doth cover thee
Is but the seemly raiment of my heart,
Which in thy breast doth live, as thine in me.
How can I then be elder than thou art?
O therefore, love, be of thyself so wary
As I not for myself but for thee will,
Bearing thy heart, which I will keep so chary
As tender nurse her babe from faring ill:
    Presume not on thy heart when mine is slain;
    Thou gav'st me thine, not to give back again.

二二

我的镜子不能使我承认老朽[19]，
只消青春能与你一同常驻；
但是看到时间在你额上留下犁沟，
我就要提防死将把我的一生结束。
因为你所拥有的一切的美丽，
只像是我的心所披上的服装，
我的心住在你胸里，你的心住在我胸里。
我如何能是比你更为年长？
所以呀，朋友，你要珍重自己，
像我不为我自己而为你那样地珍重。
怀抱着你的心，我要小心翼翼，
像是慈爱的乳母维护她的孩婴。
　　我心一死，莫想把你的心再收回去。
　　你已把心给了我，我不能再还给你。

Sonnet 23

As an unperfect actor on the stage,
Who with his fear is put besides his part,
Or some fierce thing replete with too much rage,
Whose strength's abundance weakens his own heart;
So I, for fear of trust, forget to say
The perfect ceremony of love's rite,
And in mine own love's strength seem to decay,
O'ercharged with burthen of mine own love's might:
O let my looks be then the eloquence
And dumb presagers of my speaking breast,
Who plead for love, and look for recompense,
More than that tongue that more hath more expressed.
 O learn to read what silent love hath writ:
 To hear with eyes belongs to love's fine wit.

二三

像是舞台上的一个笨拙的演员，
惊慌中忘记了他的戏词；
又像是一只野兽过度地凶残，
雄厚的威力削弱了内心的控制；
所以，我，缺乏自信，忘了说
成篇大套的爱情的辞令。
自己爱得太狠，反倒觉得虚弱，
爱的力量把我压得太沉重。
啊，让我这哑口无声的诗卷
像哑剧一般为我表达满腔的言语[20]，
为我去求爱，为我讨对方的喜欢，
比能言善道的舌头更能畅达情意。
　　请试读无言之爱所发出来的呼声，
　　用眼睛来听该是情人应有的本领。

Sonnet 24

Mine eye hath played the painter and hath stelled
Thy beauty's form in table of my heart;
My body is the frame wherein 'tis held,
And pèrspective it is best painter's art,
For through the painter must you see his skill
To find where your true image pictured lies,
Which in my bosom's shop is hanging still,
That hath his windows glazèd with thine eyes.
Now see what good turns eyes for eyes have done:
Mine eyes have drawn thy shape, and thine for me
Are windows to my breast, wherethrough the sun
Delights to peep, to gaze therein on thee.
    Yet eyes this cunning want to grace their art,
    They draw but what they see, know not the heart.

二四

我的眼睛权充一个画家，
把你的美貌刻画在我的心版上；
我的身体便是那张画的框架，
透过我的眼睛才能看到最美的画像[21]。
你必须透过我的眼睛才能看到画家的绝技，
因为你的真正的肖像是画在那个地方，
那肖像是永远悬挂在我的心房里，
你的眼睛便是那心房的玻璃窗。
请看眼睛对眼睛多么互相有用处，
我的眼画了你的像，你的眼
为我的胸膛开了窗。经过那窗户，
太阳喜欢对着你窥探。
　　但是眼睛在艺术上还欠缺一点技能，
　　只能画所看到的东西，不能体会心灵。

Sonnet 25

Let those who are in favour with their stars
Of public honour and proud titles boast,
Whilst I, whom fortune of such triumph bars,
Unlooked for joy in that I honour most.
Great princes' favourites their fair leaves spread
But as the marigold at the sun's eye,
And in themselves their pride lies burièd,
For at a frown they in their glory die.
The painful warrior famousèd for fight,
After a thousand victories once foiled,
Is from the book of honour rasèd quite,
And all the rest forgot for which he toiled:
    Then happy I that love and am belovèd
    Where I may not remove, nor be removèd.

二五

让吉星高照之下的那些人们

夸耀他们的高官显爵，

这种好运固然于我无份，

从我最敬爱的人我却得到了喜悦。

帝王宠幸的人们像金盏草，

只是朝着太阳展瓣，

刹时间要收起他们的骄傲，

帝王眉头一皱，他们的光荣就会消散。

以善战著名的忠勇之士，

千次胜利之后只要打败一回，

光荣的史册便要注销他的名字，

以往的勋绩全部地付诸流水。

　　我爱人并且被人爱，我好运气，

　　我不见异思迁，亦不虞被人抛弃。

Sonnet 26

Lord of my love, to whom in vassalage
Thy merit hath my duty strongly knit,
To thee I send this written ambassage
To witness duty, not to show my wit;
Duty so great, which wit so poor as mine
May make seem bare, in wanting words to show it,
But that I hope some good conceit of thine
In thy soul's thought (all naked) will bestow it,
Till whatsoever star that guides my moving
Points on me graciously with fair aspèct,
And puts apparel on my tottered loving,
To show me worthy of thy sweet respect:
Then may I dare to boast how I do love thee,
Till then, not show my head where thou mayst prove me.

二六[22]

我爱情的主宰哟，你的优点
值得使我对你永效忠诚，
我呈上这些作品到你身边，
是表示恭顺，不是炫耀才能。
我的才气不足，词不达意，
使得我的忠诚表示显得寒酸。
我希望你能看过心中欢喜，
接受我这些简陋的诗篇。
有一天，导引我的一颗星宿
照着我走上一帆风顺的途程，
给我的褴褛的爱穿上华丽的衣服，
使我值得接受你的爱敬[23]：
　　那时节我才夸口我对你如何眷恋，
　　在那之前我不敢出头受你的考验。

Sonnet 27

Weary with toil, I haste me to my bed,
The dear repose for limbs with travel tired,
But then begins a journey in my head
To work my mind, when body's work's expired;
For then my thoughts (from far where I abide)
Intend a zealous pilgrimage to thee,
And keep my drooping eyelids open wide,
Looking on darkness which the blind do see;
Save that my soul's imaginary sight
Presents thy shadow to my sightless view,
Which like a jewel (hung in ghastly night)
Makes black night beauteous, and her old face new.
Lo thus by day my limbs, by night my mind,
For thee, and for myself, no quiet find.

二七[24]

奔波得疲倦了，我赶快爬上床铺，
那是旅途劳顿的肢体休息之所；
但是我的脑子里又走上了一段路，
肉体的劳作停止，心里又要振作；
因为我的情思，从这遥远的所在，
动身前去和你热烈地会面，
使我沉重的眼皮睁得大开，
呆望着盲人们眼前的一片黑暗；
只是我的灵魂之富于幻想的眼睛，
在一片黑暗中看到了你的影像，
恰似一颗宝石悬在漆黑的半天空，
使得黑暗变美，另是一番新的模样。
　　看，白天我的肢体，夜里我的心灵，
　　为了想你，为了奔波，永不得安宁。

Sonnet 28

How can I then return in happy plight
That am debarred the benefit of rest?
When day's oppression is not eased by night,
But day by night and night by day oppressed;
And each (though enemies to either's reign)
Do in consent shake hands to torture me,
The one by toil, the other to complain
How far I toil, still farther off from thee.
I tell the day to please him thou art bright,
And dost him grace when clouds do blot the heaven;
So flatter I the swart–complexioned night,
When sparkling stars twire not thou gild'st the even:
  But day doth daily draw my sorrows longer,
  And night doth nightly make griefs' length seem stronger.

二八

我如何能容光焕发地归去，
既然一点休息也不能得到？
白昼的辛劳，夜里不得休息，
夜以继日日以继夜地受着煎熬。
日与夜，彼此原是敌人，
却携手合作把我来虐待，
一个令我奔波，一个令我怨恨，
如此奔波还是和你这样远地离开。
为了讨好，我对白昼说，你真光明，
乌云蔽天的时候你照得它通亮；
同样地我对黑夜也极力奉承，
星不眨眼的时候你把它镀成金的一样。
　　但是白昼一天天地把我的愁苦拖长，
　　夜晚每晚都更加重我的悲伤。

Sonnet 29

When in disgrace with Fortune and men's eyes,
I all alone beweep my outcast state,
And trouble deaf heaven with my bootless cries,
And look upon myself and curse my fate,
Wishing me like to one more rich in hope,
Featured like him, like him with friends possessed,
Desiring this man's art, and that man's scope,
With what I most enjoy contented least;
Yet in these thoughts myself almost despising,
Haply I think on thee, and then my state
(Like to the lark at break of day arising
From sullen earth) sings hymns at heaven's gate;
  For thy sweet love remember'd such wealth brings
  That then I scorn to change my state with kings.

二九

我遭幸运之神和世人的白眼,
便独自哭我这身世的飘零,
以无益的哀号惊动耳聋的青天,
看着自己, 咒骂我的苦命,
愿自己能像某人之前途光明,
有某人的仪表, 有某人广大的交际,
羡慕这一个的文笔, 那一个才气纵横,
对于自己的这一份最不满意;
但是这样想来想去, 几乎轻蔑我自己,
偶然想起了你——那时节的我
恰似破晓时云雀从地面飞起,
在天门引吭高歌。
　　想起了你的爱, 那真是财富无限,
　　虽南面王的地位我亦不屑于交换。

Sonnet 30

When to the sessions of sweet silent thought
I summon up remembrance of things past,
I sigh the lack of many a thing I sought,
And with old woes new wail my dear time's waste;
Then can I drown an eye (unused to flow)
For precious friends hid in death's dateless night,
And weep afresh love's long since cancelled woe,
And moan th'expense of many a vanished sight;
Then can I grieve at grievances foregone,
And heavily from woe to woe tell o'er
The sad account of fore–bemoanèd moan,
Which I new pay as if not paid before:
    But if the while I think on thee (dear friend)
    All losses are restored, and sorrows end.

三〇

当我召唤往事的回忆
前来甜蜜默想的公堂，
我为许多追求未遂的事物而叹息，
为被时间毁灭的亲人而再度哀伤，
向不流泪的眼睛就要泪如泉涌，
因为多少好友均已幽冥永隔，
要重温早已勾销的爱情的苦痛，
哀叹多少往事一去而不可复得。
我为以往的悲苦而再感悲苦，
把以往的痛心的事情
一件一件地从头细数，
好像旧债未还，现在才偿清。
　　但是我如果想到你，亲爱的朋友，
　　一切损失都恢复，结束一切的哀愁。

Sonnet 31

Thy bosom is endearèd with all hearts,
Which I by lacking have supposèd dead,
And there reigns love and all love's loving parts,
And all those friends which I thought burièd.
How many a holy and obsequious tear
Hath dear religious love stol'n from mine eye,
As interest of the dead, which now appear
But things removed that hidden in thee lie!
Thou art the grave where buried love doth live,
Hung with the trophies of my lovers gone,
Who all their parts of me to thee did give;
That due of many now is thine alone.
    Their images I loved I view in thee,
    And thou (all they) hast all the all of me.

三一 [25]

许多阔别的知交，我以为早已死去，
原来都是在你的胸膛里面聚首，
那里洋溢着友爱，一切的殷勤好意，
以及我认为已经埋葬了的那些朋友。
深挚神圣的友爱从我的眼里
偷去了多少圣洁哀悼的眼泪，
那泪好像是死者应得的权益，
其实他们只是搬到了你的胸膛之内。
你是一座坟，里面住着死去的友人，
我的亡友们的纪念物挂在上面，
他们把我的情意都送给你收存，
他们应得的友谊现在为你独占：
　　在你身上我看到他们的遗容，
　　你是他们全体，你得到我全部友情。

Sonnet 32

If thou survive my well–contented day,
When that churl Death my bones with dust shall cover,
And shalt by fortune once more re–survey
These poor rude lines of thy deceasèd lover,
Compare them with the bett'ring of the time,
And though they be outstripped by every pen,
Reserve them for my love, not for their rhyme,
Exceeded by the height of happier men.
O then vouchsafe me but this loving thought:
'Had my friend's Muse grown with this growing age,
A dearer birth than this his love had brought
To march in ranks of better equipage:
But since he died, and poets better prove,
Theirs for their style I'll read, his for his love.'

三二

如果“死亡”那贱人用黄土埋我的骸骨[26]，
我了无遗憾地死去，而你尚在人间，
而且偶然地再度来阅读
你的亡友的拙劣的诗篇，
若拿来和时下进步的诗人相比，
纵然每个人的作品都比我的强，
每个人都比我有更高的造诣，
为了爱，不为艺术，请保存我这些诗章。
啊，我盼你对我有这样的想法：
“我的朋友的诗才若能随着时代成熟，
他的友爱必能表现出更高的才华，
在更辉煌的诗人行列中向前迈步。
　　可惜他已死去，别的诗人都进步了，
　　我读他们是赏其文笔，读他是为不忘旧好。”

Sonnet 33

Full many a glorious morning have I seen
Flatter the mountain tops with sovereign eye,
Kissing with golden face the meadows green,
Gilding pale streams with heavenly alcumy,
Anon permit the basest clouds to ride
With ugly rack on his celestial face,
And from the fòrlorn world his visage hide,
Stealing unseen to west with this disgrace:
Even so my sun one early morn did shine
With all triumphant splendour on my brow;
But out alack, he was but one hour mine,
The region cloud hath masked him from me now.
　Yet him for this my love no whit disdaineth:
　Suns of the world may stain, when heaven's sun staineth.

三三 [27]

我曾见过多少次灿烂的清晨
以帝王的眼光宠顾着山巅，
以金赤的脸吻那油绿的草茵，
以奇妙的幻术镀亮灰色的河川；
忽然竟任由卑贱的云雾
挟着阴霾在他脸上逡巡，
使凄凉的世界看不见他的面目，
含着羞悄悄地西沉。
有一天早晨我的太阳也是这样，
光芒四射地照耀着我的脸。
但是，哎呀，他属于我不过是片刻时光，
现在乌云蔽空已经把他遮掩。
　　我的爱却不因此而对他冷淡，
　　天上太阳都会变色，地上的何尝不然。

Sonnet 34

Why didst thou promise such a beauteous day,
And make me travel forth without my cloak,
To let base clouds o'ertake me in my way,
Hiding thy brav'ry in their rotten smoke?
'Tis not enough that through the cloud thou break,
To dry the rain on my storm–beaten face,
For no man well of such a salve can speak,
That heals the wound, and cures not the disgrace:
Nor can thy shame give physic to my grief;
Though thou repent, yet I have still the loss:
Th'offender's sorrow lends but weak relief
To him that bears the strong offence's cross.
  Ah, but those tears are pearl which thy love sheeds,
  And they are rich, and ransom all ill deeds.

三四

你为什么对我预示天气晴朗，
使我不带外衣就走上了征途，
半途中却让乌云把我赶上，
把你的光芒隐入蒙蒙的云雾？
你纵然冲破云层晒干我脸上的雨点，
那对我也没有多大的好处，
因为没有人肯称赞
只疗创伤而不医心病的药物。
何况你的羞惭也治不了我的伤心，
你虽然悔过，我的损失无法补偿。
害人者的愁苦对于受害的人
所身受的荼毒没有多大救济的力量。
　　但是你的爱所洒珍珠一般的泪，
　　价值连城，足以赎一切的罪。

Sonnet 35

No more be grieved at that which thou hast done:
Roses have thorns, and silver fountains mud,
Clouds and eclipses stain both moon and sun,
And loathsome canker lives in sweetest bud.
All men make faults, and even I in this,
Authorizing thy trespass with compare,
Myself corrupting salving thy amiss,
Excusing thy sins more than their sins are;
For to thy sensual fault I bring in sense –
Thy adverse party is thy advocate –
And 'gainst myself a lawful plea commence:
Such civil war is in my love and hate
    That I an àccessary needs must be
    To that sweet thief which sourly robs from me.

三五

不必再为你做下的事而悲伤：
玫瑰有刺，银色泉源会变浊，
云翳亏蚀也能遮暗月亮太阳，
最娇媚的花苞偏有虫儿来蛀。
人孰无过，我自己也是有错的，
我妄用比喻为你开脱罪行，
为掩饰你的过失而我自陷于无理，
将物比人，未免过分地矫情[28]。
因为我强词夺理地开脱你的肉欲，
你的对手方成了你的辩护人。
我要开始申诉正式控告我自己：
我的爱与恨是如此地自相矛盾，
　　以至于自己成为一名共犯了，
　　帮助了那狠心劫掠我的风流强盗。

Sonnet 36

Let me confess that we two must be twain,
Although our undivided loves are one:
So shall those blots that do with me remain,
Without thy help, by me be borne alone.
In our two loves there is but one respect,
Though in our lives a separable spite,
Which though it alter not love's sole effect,
Yet doth it steal sweet hours from love's delight.
I may not evermore acknowledge thee,
Lest my bewailèd guilt should do thee shame,
Nor thou with public kindness honour me,
Unless thou take that honour from thy name:
    But do not so; I love thee in such sort,
    As thou being mine, mine is thy good report.

三六[29]

我要承认我们两个必须分散，
虽然我们有不可分割的一段情，
好让那耻辱留在我的身畔，
不需你帮助，让我独自来担承。
虽然命运打击我们，必须分离，
我们两个的爱却是一致的，
命运改变不了我们的爱的专一，
却能把爱的欢乐时间抢夺了去。
我永远不能再和你过从，
否则我的罪过会要把你连累；
你也不必再公然给我以恩宠，
除非你甘愿辱没你的门楣。
　　但不可那样做，我爱你如此之深，
　　你是我的，你的名声也该为我保存。

Sonnet 37

As a decrepit father takes delight
To see his active child do deeds of youth,
So I, made lame by Fortune's dearest spite,
Take all my comfort of thy worth and truth;
For whether beauty, birth, or wealth, or wit,
Or any of these all, or all, or more,
Intitled in thy parts, do crownèd sit,
I make my love ingrafted to this store:
So then I am not lame, poor, nor despised,
Whilst that this shadow doth such substance give,
That I in thy abundance am sufficed,
And by a part of all thy glory live:
  Look what is best, that best I wish in thee;
  This wish I have, then ten times happy me.

三七

像是衰老的父亲欢欢喜喜地看着
他的活泼的孩子青年有为，
我，受了命运的残酷折磨，
从你的高贵精明而获得安慰。
无论仪表、门第、财产或聪明，
或任何一项，或全部，或更多项目，
你都能表现得十分出众。
我把爱的枝条接上你那丰美的根株，
于是我便不苦、不穷，不受人白眼。
这一番想象竟给了我真实的资料，
我满意于你这一份丰盛的资产，
我借你的一部分光荣而自在逍遥。
　　人间的至善至美，我愿都属于你。
　　我这愿望达成了，所以十倍地快活如意！

Sonnet 38

How can my Muse want subject to invent
While thou dost breathe, that pour'st into my verse
Thine own sweet argument, too excellent
For every vulgar paper to rehearse?
O give thyself the thanks if aught in me
Worthy perusal stand against thy sight,
For who's so dumb that cannot write to thee,
When thou thyself dost give invention light?
Be thou the tenth Muse, ten times more in worth
Than those old nine which rhymers invocate,
And he that calls on thee, let him bring forth
Eternal numbers to outlive long date.
    If my slight Muse do please these curious days,
    The pain be mine, but thine shall be the praise.

三八

我的“诗神”的吟咏资料不虞缺少，
只要你活着，你就会把你自身的题材
注入我的诗篇，你自身的美妙
岂是每个庸碌的诗人所能描写得来?
我的诗若有几句值得你看一眼，
啊，你该感谢的是你自己，
因为你自己引起别人的灵感，
谁那样笨不写诗献给你?
任由诗人乞灵的“诗神”原有九个，
你做第十个吧，你有十倍的力量。
现在有人向你呼唤，你让他创作
一些万古常新的不朽的诗章。
　　拙诗若能博得苛求的读者欣赏，
　　我不辞辛劳，让你接受赞扬。

Sonnet 39

O how thy worth with manners may I sing,
When thou art all the better part of me?
What can mine own praise to mine own self bring?
And what is't but mine own when I praise thee?
Even for this, let us divided live,
And our dear love lose name of single one,
That by this separation I may give
That due to thee which thou deserv'st alone.
O absence, what a torment wouldst thou prove,
Were it not thy sour leisure gave sweet leave
To entertain the time with thoughts of love,
Which time and thoughts so sweetly dost deceive,
    And that thou teachest how to make one twain,
    By praising him here who doth hence remain.

三九

啊，你是我的较佳一半的全部，
我怎能适当地赞美你呢？
我自己吹嘘对我自己有何益处，
我赞美你岂不就是赞美我自己？
因此之故，我们也就该分散，
我们的爱只是损失正团聚之名，
我们分离之后我便可以贡献
你所应独得的一份奉承。
啊，别离呀，你将是一场何等苦难，
若非你这惨痛的机缘能允许我
以两地相思来打发时间，
因为相思最能把时间与愁怀来消磨，
　　并且你教我如何把一个人分为两份，
　　在诗里赞美一个远在异方的人。

Sonnet 40

Take all my loves, my love, yea, take them all;
What hast thou then more than thou hadst before?
No love, my love, that thou mayst true love call;
All mine was thine, before thou hadst this more.
Then if for my love thou my love receivest,
I cannot blame thee for my love thou usest;
But yet be blamed, if thou this self deceivest
By wilful taste of what thy self refusest.
I do forgive thy robb'ry, gentle thief,
Although thou steal thee all my poverty;
And yet love knows it is a greater grief
To bear love's wrong than hate's known injury.
    Lascivious grace, in whom all ill well shows,
    Kill me with spites, yet we must not be foes.

四〇

把我爱的都拿去，爱人，都拿去。
在你以前所有的之外还能有什么增加?
你夺去的爱不会是真实的情意，
你夺得这个之前，我的一切都属你啦。
如果你为了爱我而接收我的爱人，
我不怪你和我的爱人缱绻。
可是还要怪你，如果你纡贵屈尊，
和一个你所不爱的女人胡缠。
我宽恕你的劫夺，风流强盗，
虽然你夺了我仅有的这一点点。
不过情场中人都会知晓，
忍受爱的委曲比恨的创伤更为悲惨。
　　放荡的公子，你显露了一切的劣迹，
　　你尽管辱我杀我，我们不可成为仇敌。

Sonnet 41

Those pretty wrongs that liberty commits,
When I am sometime absent from thy heart,
Thy beauty and thy years full well befits,
For still temptation follows where thou art.
Gentle thou art, and therefore to be won,
Beauteous thou art, therefore to be assailed;
And when a woman woos, what woman's son
Will sourly leave her till he have prevailed?
Ay me, but yet thou mightst my seat forbear,
And chide thy beauty and thy straying youth,
Who lead thee in their riot even there
Where thou art forced to break a twofold truth:
　Hers, by thy beauty tempting her to thee,
　Thine, by thy beauty being false to me.

四一

有时我不在你的身边，
你做出一些小小的荒唐，
你年轻貌美，难怪其然，
你在哪里都有诱惑的力量：
你高贵温柔，所以令人艳羡；
你仪表堂堂，所以招人略诱；
女人献媚，哪个女人生的男子汉
能够峻拒，不令她勾引到手？
哎呀，你可以不霸占我的地位，
你应当谴责你的青春美貌
不该引诱你胡作非为，
逼你把双重的誓约毁掉。
　　她的誓约，因你的美貌而诱她失身；
　　你的誓约，因你的美貌而对我负心。

Sonnet 42

That thou hast her, it is not all my grief,
And yet it may be said I loved her dearly;
That she hath thee is of my wailing chief,
A loss in love that touches me more nearly.
Loving offenders, thus I will excuse ye:
Thou dost love her because thou know'st I love her,
And for my sake even so doth she abuse me,
Suff'ring my friend for my sake to approve her.
If I lose thee, my loss is my love's gain,
And losing her, my friend hath found that loss;
Both find each other, and I lose both twain,
And both for my sake lay on me this cross.
    But here's the joy, my friend and I are one.
    Sweet flattery! then she loves but me alone.

四二

你占有她，那不是我全部的痛苦，
不过我确是对她有深深的爱；
她占有你，那才是我痛苦主要的缘故，
使我感触更深的友谊失败。
亲爱的罪人，我愿这样地为你们开脱：
你爱她，因为你知道我对她钟情；
她也是为我的缘故才欺骗我，
让我的朋友为我的缘故而把她看中[30]。
我失去你，我的损失正是我的爱人的收益；
我失去她，这损失正被我的朋友所寻获；
你们互有所得，我是二者俱行失去，
你们折磨我都是为了我的缘故。
　　但是我乐观，我的朋友和我原是一个。
　　悦耳的自欺之谈！她爱的只是我。

Sonnet 43

When most I wink, then do mine eyes best see,
For all the day they view things unrespected;
But when I sleep, in dreams they look on thee,
And darkly bright, are bright in dark directed.
Then thou, whose shadow shadows doth make bright,
How would thy shadow's form form happy show
To the clear day with thy much clearer light,
When to unseeing eyes thy shade shines so!
How would (I say) mine eyes be blessèd made,
By looking on thee in the living day,
When in dead night thy fair imperfect shade
Through heavy sleep on sightless eyes doth stay!
  All days are nights to see till I see thee,
  And nights bright days when dreams do show thee me.

四三[31]

我闭上眼，我看得最清晰，
因为在白昼一切都视若无睹；
但是到了睡时梦中看到你，
衷心喜悦，黑暗中看得最清楚[32]。
你的影像把黑暗照得通亮，
幽灵既能这样照耀闭着的双眼，
那么你的真身有比白昼更强的光芒，
将使白昼显得何等地格外灿烂[33]！
在深夜中你的残缺的美丽影像
能穿过熟睡来到没视力的眼前，
我若在大清白昼对着你望，
对于我的眼睛那将是何等的福缘！
　　看不到你，白昼有如黑夜什么也看不见；
　　黑夜有如白昼，如果你在梦中出现。

Sonnet 44

If the dull substance of my flesh were thought,
Injurious distance should not stop my way,
For then despite of space I would be brought,
From limits far remote, where thou dost stay.
No matter then although my foot did stand
Upon the farthest earth removed from thee,
For nimble thought can jump both sea and land
As soon as think the place where he would be.
But ah, thought kills me that I am not thought,
To leap large lengths of miles when thou art gone,
But that, so much of earth and water wrought,
I must attend time's leisure with my moan,
    Receiving nought by elements so slow
    But heavy tears, badges of either's woe.

四四

我的陋质顽躯若能像思想一般轻灵[34]，
残酷的距离便不能拦阻我。
那时节我会不顾遥远的路程，
从遥远的地方飞到你的住所。
纵然我站立在离你最远的地方，
到那时节也就没有什么关系。
因为轻灵的思想能跳过陆地与海洋，
一想你在何方，立即到达那里。
但是呀，我不是思想，实在遗憾无穷，
你去后我并不能飞越万里，
我乃是土与水混合而成，
只好悲伤地恳求“时间”准我们团聚。
　　我是由这样卑贱的两种元素做成的，
　　只能求得忧伤的泪，我的元素之悲哀的标帜。

Sonnet 45

The other two, slight air and purging fire,
Are both with thee, wherever I abide;
The first my thought, the other my desire,
These present–absent with swift motion slide;
For when these quicker elements are gone
In tender embassy of love to thee,
My life, being made of four, with two alone
Sinks down to death, oppressed with melancholy,
Until life's composition be recured
By those swift messengers returned from thee,
Who even but now come back again assured
Of thy fair health, recounting it to me.
    This told, I joy, but then no longer glad,
    I send them back again and straight grow sad.

四五

我另外二元素，轻灵的气与净化的火，
无论我在何处，都是跟着你在一起。
前者是我的思想，我的情感是后者，
二者都动作敏捷地倏来倏去。
因为这两个敏捷的元素
前去代我向你殷勤做爱之际，
组成我这生命的四个元素仅余半数，
忧郁重压之下，只得消沉而死。
等那敏捷使者从你那里归来，
把我的生命的组织复原，
就在这时节他们已经返回，
对我声言你的身体康安。
　　我听了高兴，可是高兴不了多久，
　　我又把他们遣回，立刻开始忧愁。

Sonnet 46

Mine eye and heart are at a mortal war,
How to divide the conquest of thy sight:
Mine eye my heart thy picture's sight would bar,
My heart mine eye the freedom of that right.
My heart doth plead that thou in him dost lie
(A closet never pierced with crystal eyes),
But the defendant doth that plea deny,
And says in him thy fair appearance lies.
To 'cide this title is impanellèd
A quest of thoughts, all tenants to the heart,
And by their verdict is determinèd
The clear eye's moiety and the dear heart's part,
As thus: mine eye's due is thy outward part,
And my heart's right thy inward love of heart.

四六[35]

我的眼和心拼命地相争，

争着分享看你的权利：

我的眼不准我的心看你的图形，

我的心拒绝我的眼独占那项权益；

我的心说，你是在他心里藏着，

那是锐眼永远看不穿的一个房间；

但是被告否认这项诉说，

他说你的容颜只能由他来观看。

为了解决这项权利纠纷，

住在心中的思想应聘为陪审团，

由于他们的判决而获得结论，

眼该分到多少，心该获得若干。

　　是这样的：我的眼可享受你的外形，

　　我的心占有你的内在的爱情。

Sonnet 47

Betwixt mine eye and heart a league is took,
And each doth good turns now unto the other:
When that mine eye is famished for a look,
Or heart in love with sighs himself doth smother,
With my love's picture then my eye doth feast,
And to the painted banquet bids my heart;
Another time mine eye is my heart's guest,
And in his thoughts of love doth share a part.
So either by thy picture or my love,
Thyself, away, are present still with me,
For thou not farther than my thoughts canst move,
And I am still with them, and they with thee;
　Or if they sleep, thy picture in my sight
　Awakes my heart to heart's and eye's delight.

四七

我的眼与心和解成立，

如今彼此互相帮助：

我的眼渴望看你之际，

或心为相思而被叹息噎住，

我的眼便把吾爱的肖像饱餐一顿，

并且邀心同享这彩绘的筵席；

有时我的眼是我的心的来宾，

分享他的一部分缠绵情意。

于是靠了你的肖像或我的爱，

你虽远出仍和在我身边一般。

因为你走不出我的思想范围之外，

我永远跟着思想，思想跟在你身边。

　　如果思想睡觉，你的肖像在我眼前

　　会唤醒我，使我的心与眼享受一番。

Sonnet 48

How careful was I, when I took my way,
Each trifle under truest bars to thrust,
That to my use it might un–usèd stay
From hands of falsehood, in sure wards of trust!
But thou, to whom my jewels trifles are,
Most worthy comfort, now my greatest grief,
Thou best of dearest, and mine only care,
Art left the prey of every vulgar thief.
Thee have I not locked up in any chest,
Save where thou art not, though I feel thou art,
Within the gentle closure of my breast,
From whence at pleasure thou mayst come and part;
    And even thence thou wilt be stol'n, I fear,
    For truth proves thievish for a prize so dear.

四八 [36]

我外出时多么小心翼翼，
每件小东西都严封固扃，
放在妥当的地方来藏起，
不让心术不正的人摸去乱用！
但是你，珠宝比起你来不值一文，
我最大的安慰，也是最大的忧伤，
你是我最亲密的，我唯一挂心的人，
会成为每个市井无赖猎取的对象。
我没有把你在任何箱子里锁起，
除了我这个温暖的胸膛，
你不在里面，而我觉得你在那里，
你可以在那里自由出入地游荡。
　　从那里，我仍怕你被人偷走，
　　有这样的宝物，君子人也会下手。

Sonnet 49

Against that time (if ever that time come)
When I shall see thee frown on my defècts,
Whenas thy love hath cast his utmost sum,
Called to that audit by advised respects;
Against that time when thou shalt strangely pass,
And scarcely greet me with that sun, thine eye,
When love converted from the thing it was
Shall reasons find of settled gravity:
Against that time do I insconce me here
Within the knowledge of mine own desert,
And this my hand against myself uprear,
To guard the lawful reasons on thy part.
    To leave poor me thou hast the strength of laws,
    Since why to love I can allege no cause.

四九

为了提防那一天（如果那天真会来到），
我看着你对我的缺点狞眉皱眼，
你的爱把最后一笔款也已经付了，
精思熟虑之后要和我进行清算[37]；
为了提防那一天，你会冷冷地离去，
不肯用你那太阳似的眼睛对我一顾，
爱情变了，不再有往常的那种情意，
更何患找不出理由变得那样地严肃；
为了提防那一天，我要寻个隐蔽处，
先对自己的缺点做一番反省，
然后举起手来把我自己保护[38]，
抵抗你那振振有词的指控。
　　你有合法的权利把可怜的我抛弃，
　　因为我根本找不到令你垂爱的根据。

Sonnet 50

How heavy do I journey on the way,
When what I seek (my weary travel's end)
Doth teach that ease and that repose to say,
'Thus far the miles are measured from thy friend.'
The beast that bears me, tirèd with my woe,
Plods dully on, to bear that weight in me,
As if by some instìnct the wretch did know
His rider loved not speed being made from thee:
The bloody spur cannot provoke him on
That sometimes anger thrusts into his hide,
Which heavily he answers with a groan
More sharp to me than spurring to his side;
For that same groan doth put this in my mind:
My grief lies onward and my joy behind.

五〇

我在征途中心情多么愁苦，
我一心企求早日到达目标，
而每日安歇偏偏向我声诉：
“你离开朋友又多数里之遥。”
我的坐骑，受我愁苦的折磨，
驮着我的沉重心情缓缓走去，
这可怜东西好像本能地觉得
骑他的人不喜欢太快地离开你。
我有时怒起，踢刺他的腹部，
血淋淋的刺马钉不能使他前冲，
他只是哀鸣一声作为沉痛的答复。
他使我心伤，比我踢得他更痛，
　　因为那声哀鸣把我的心事勾起。
　　我以后全是悲哀，欢欣已成过去。

Sonnet 51

Thus can my love excuse the slow offence
Of my dull bearer, when from thee I speed:
From where thou art, why should I haste me thence?
Till I return, of posting is no need.
O what excuse will my poor beast then find,
When swift extremity can seem but slow?
Then should I spur though mounted on the wind,
In wingèd speed no motion shall I know:
Then can no horse with my desire keep pace;
Therefore desire (of perfect'st love being made)
Shall neigh (no dull flesh) in his fiery race,
But love, for love, thus shall excuse my jade:
    Since from thee going he went wilful slow,
    Towards thee I'll run and give him leave to go.

五一

为了爱，在我离你而去的时候
我会这样原谅我的马的迟缓，
我在离你而去为什么要匆匆驰骤？
除非是归来，无须急忙地把路赶。
那时最高速度还会嫌太慢，
这可怜的畜牲将如何得到宽容？
纵然驭风而行我还要催马急窜，
风驰电掣我也会觉得丝毫未动。
没有马能和我的情意并驾齐驱，
所以我这一番纯爱所做成的情意
会要奋跃嘶鸣，不同于驽骀下驷。
但是爱，由于慈悲，会原谅我的马匹[39]：
　　“当初离开你，他曾故意慢慢走，
　　我如今放脚奔向你，放他慢步优游。”

Sonnet 52

So am I as the rich whose blessèd key
Can bring him to his sweet up–lockèd treasure,
The which he will not ev’ry hour survey,
For blunting the fine point of seldom pleasure.
Therefore are feasts so solemn and so rare,
Since, seldom coming, in the long year set,
Like stones of worth they thinly placèd are,
Or captain jewels in the carcanet.
So is the time that keeps you as my chest,
Or as the wardrobe which the robe doth hide,
To make some special instant special blest,
By new unfolding his imprisoned pride.
    Blessèd are you whose worthiness gives scope,
    Being had, to triumph, being lacked, to hope.

五二

我恰似一位富翁，有一把钥匙，
能打开他锁着的可爱的宝藏，
他并不愿随时地去开启检视，
生怕难得的乐趣变得稀松平常。
所以盛大的节日必定很稀少，
难得一遇，在漫长的岁月中间
偶然一见，有如稀世的珠宝，
或几颗主要宝石镶在颈链上边。
时间，像是我的宝库，收藏着你，
又像收藏服装的一只衣箱，
只有在一些特殊的日子里
才抖出它藏着的漂亮服装。
　　你有福，你的优点实在太广泛。
　　见面时，我欢欣；不见时，我想见。

Sonnet 53

What is your substance, whereof are you made,
That millions of strange shadows on you tend,
Since every one hath, every one, one shade,
And you, but one, can every shadow lend?
Describe Adonis, and the counterfeit
Is poorly imitated after you;
On Helen's cheek all art of beauty set,
And you in Grecian tires are painted new;
Speak of the spring and foison of the year:
The one doth shadow of your beauty show,
The other as your bounty doth appear,
And you in every blessèd shape we know.
    In all external grace you have some part,
    But you like none, none you, for constant heart.

五三

你究竟是什么原料所造成，

有万千的影子跟随着你？

每一个人只能有一个阴影，

你，一个人，却各种影子都能供给：

描绘阿都尼斯，那幅画像

将是你的肖像之失败的作品；

把一切绘画手段集中在海伦脸上，

结果是你穿着希腊服装的新像一帧[40]。

讲起一年之间的春华秋实，

前者象征你的容光照出的阴影，

后者像是你的乐善好施。

我们看出你具有各种优美的态形。

　　一切仪表的美都是属于你的，

　　但是讲到不变的心，没人能和你比。

Sonnet 54

O how much more doth beauty beauteous seem
By that sweet ornament which truth doth give!
The rose looks fair, but fairer we it deem
For that sweet odour which doth in it live.
The canker blooms have full as deep a dye
As the perfumèd tincture of the roses,
Hang on such thorns, and play as wantonly,
When summer's breath their maskèd buds discloses;
But, for their virtue only is their show,
They live unwooed, and unrespected fade,
Die to themselves. Sweet roses do not so,
Of their sweet deaths are sweetest odours made:
　And so of you, beauteous and lovely youth,
　When that shall vade, by verse distils your truth.

五四

美貌将显得多么格外地美，
若是加上忠诚做美妙的装潢！
玫瑰好看，但是我们以为
使他格外好看的是那一缕芬芳。
野蔷薇和那芳香的玫瑰
有同样秾丽的颜色，
夏日熏风吹破他们的蓓蕾，
同样地高挂枝头，同样地快乐。
只因他的妙处全在于仪表，
便没有人爱没有人理地凋谢，
悄悄地死去。玫瑰便不然了，
从死之中炼出最可爱的香液。
　　你也是一样，美貌可爱的少年，
　　你青春消逝，你的忠诚由诗提炼。

Sonnet 55

Not marble nor the gilded monuments
Of princes shall outlive this pow'rful rhyme,
But you shall shine more bright in these contènts
Than unswept stone, besmeared with sluttish time.
When wasteful war shall statues overturn,
And broils root out the work of masonry,
Nor Mars his sword nor war's quick fire shall burn
The living record of your memory.
'Gainst death and all oblivious enmity
Shall you pace forth; your praise shall still find room
Even in the eyes of all posterity
That wear this world out to the ending doom.
　So, till the Judgement that yourself arise,
　You live in this, and dwell in lovers' eyes.

五五

石碑或金碧辉煌的帝王纪念碑
不会比这有力的诗篇寿命更长。
你在这诗篇里发射出来的光辉
将比多年积尘不扫的石碑更亮。
毁灭性的战争会把雕像推翻，
打斗会把皇皇建筑连根铲除，
但是马尔斯的剑或战争的火焰[41]
不能烧掉你的名声之活的记录。
你可以不顾死亡和被人遗忘之虞，
昂然前进，你的光荣的名声
将永久存在于一切后人的眼里，
它们直到世界末日绵延无穷。
　　直到最后审判之日你再站起，
　　你活在诗里，住在情人们眼里。

Sonnet 56

Sweet love, renew thy force, be it not said
Thy edge should blunter be than appetite,
Which but today by feeding is allayed,
Tomorrow sharp'ned in his former might.
So, love, be thou: although today thou fill
Thy hungry eyes even till they wink with fullness,
Tomorrow see again, and do not kill
The spirit of love with a perpetual dullness:
Let this sad int'rim like the ocean be
Which parts the shore, where two contracted new
Come daily to the banks, that when they see
Return of love, more blest may be the view;
　As call it winter, which being full of care,
　Makes summer's welcome, thrice more wished, more rare.

五六

甜蜜的爱情，重振你的力量，
不要令人说你的锋芒比食欲钝，
今天吃饱只是今天不饿得慌，
明天依旧要饿得发狠。
爱情，你也这样吧：虽然你今天
塞饱了饿眼，塞得两眼闭拢起来，
明天要再睁开眼睛看看，
不要用永久的昏迷杀死了爱。
这昏迷期间要像海洋一般[42]，
把两个新婚的人分开两地，
他们每天来到海岸边，
看到爱潮高涨，那景况格外可喜；
　　也可以把它比作冬天，满目凄凉，
　　使得夏天格外地稀罕，令人向往。

Sonnet 57

Being your slave, what should I do but tend
Upon the hours and times of your desire?
I have no precious time at all to spend,
Nor services to do till you require.
Nor dare I chide the world-without-end hour
Whilst I (my sovereign) watch the clock for you,
Nor think the bitterness of absence sour
When you have bid your servant once adieu.
Nor dare I question with my jealous thought
Where you may be, or your affairs suppose,
But like a sad slave stay and think of nought
Save where you are how happy you make those.
    So true a fool is love that in your will
    (Though you do any thing) he thinks no ill.

五七

既是你的奴仆，我还能做什么，
除了随时随刻地听候你的差遣？
我根本没有宝贵时间可供消磨，
也没有事可做，除了听你使唤；
我不敢责骂那永无终止的时间，
我的主人，我乖乖为你守着时钟，
当你对你的奴仆说了一声再见，
我也不敢想那黯然分离的苦痛；
我满心疑虑，可是不敢追问
你在什么地方，你在做什么事情，
我像个可怜的奴才安守本分，
只是揣想和你相遇的人多么高兴。
　　痴爱的人真是蠢，随便你做什么[43]，
　　他都会觉得你的存心不恶。

Sonnet 58

That god forbid, that made me first your slave,
I should in thought control your times of pleasure,
Or at your hand th'account of hours to crave,
Being your vassal bound to stay your leisure.
O let me suffer (being at your beck)
Th'imprisoned absence of your liberty,
And patience, tame to sufferance, bide each check,
Without accusing you of injury.
Be where you list, your charter is so strong
That you yourself may privilege your time
To what you will; to you it doth belong
Yourself to pardon of self-doing crime.
    I am to wait, though waiting so be hell,
    Not blame your pleasure, be it ill or well.

五八

使我生而为你奴仆的那个神
不准我在思想中限制你的享受，
也不准我要求你计算时辰，
我是你的奴仆，只合耐心等候！
啊！我既听你呼唤，我只能够
任你放荡自由，让我忍受孤苦，
忍受惯了就会随时地逆来顺受
而不怨恨你对我的欺侮！
随心所欲地去吧，你有权利
任意支配你的时间，
时间完全是你自己的，
你自己才可原谅你自作自受的罪愆。
　　等待固然难熬，我还是要等待，
　　不敢怪你享乐，无论那是好是坏。

Sonnet 59

If there be nothing new, but that which is
Hath been before, how are our brains beguiled,
Which, labouring for invention, bear amiss
The second burthen of a former child!
O that recòrd could with a backward look,
Even of five hundred courses of the sun,
Show me your image in some àntique book,
Since mind at first in character was done,
That I might see what the old world could say
To this composèd wonder of your frame:
Whether we are mended, or whe'er better they,
Or whether revolution be the same.
  O sure I am the wits of former days
  To subjects worse have given admiring praise.

五九 [44]

如果世上无新物，一切是早已有的，
我们的头脑岂非是受了大骗，
枉自努力创造，想孕育新奇的东西，
结果生出来只是旧有产物的重现！
我愿记载往事的典籍
对五百年前旧事加以回顾，
告诉我自从文字纪事时候起，
典籍中可曾有过你这样的人物！
我愿知道古人有什么可夸，
面对着你这样翩翩的形体，
究竟我们进步，还是他们较佳，
还是变来变去都是一样的。
　　我敢说，古代有见识的人们
　　把赞颂之词送给了较劣的产品。

Sonnet 60

Like as the waves make towards the pebbled shore,
So do our minutes hasten to their end,
Each changing place with that which goes before,
In sequent toil all forwards do contend.
Nativity, once in the main of light,
Crawls to maturity, wherewith being crowned,
Crookèd eclipses 'gainst his glory fight,
And Time that gave doth now his gift confound.
Time doth transfix the flourish set on youth,
And delves the parallels in beauty's brow,
Feeds on the rarities of nature's truth,
And nothing stands but for his scythe to mow.
　And yet to times in hope my verse shall stand,
　Praising thy worth, despite his cruel hand.

六〇

像波浪向碎石的岸上冲，
人生也每分钟奔向终点，
每一分钟代替了前一分钟，
连续地努力，争着往前赶。
婴儿，一旦跃入“光海”里面，
爬到成年，把那荣冠戴起，
邪恶的蚀影便对他的光荣作战，
“时间”竟摧残它自己的赠予。
“时间”真能毁坏青春的美貌，
给美人的额上钻刻了沟纹，
把自然的杰作中的珍品吞掉，
镰刀过处，一切都荡然无存。
　　但是我的诗篇要垂诸永久，
　　赞美你的优秀，不怕它的毒手。

Sonnet 61

Is it thy will thy image should keep open
My heavy eyelids to the weary night?
Dost thou desire my slumbers should be broken,
While shadows like to thee do mock my sight?
Is it thy spirit that thou send'st from thee
So far from home into my deeds to pry,
To find out shames and idle hours in me,
The scope and tenure of thy jealousy?
O no, thy love, though much, is not so great;
It is my love that keeps mine eye awake,
Mine own true love that doth my rest defeat,
To play the watchman ever for thy sake.
    For thee watch I, whilst thou dost wake elsewhere,
    From me far off, with others all too near.

六一

是否你有意用你的影像
使我在漫长夜里睁着睡眼?
用貌似你的影子戏弄我的目光,
使得我为之彻夜地失眠?
是否你的灵魂受你的差遣,
远道而来查看我的行为状况,
在行为上有无逾闲荡检,
构成了你的嫉妒的对象?
啊, 不! 你的爱不至于这样深刻,
是我的爱使我闭不上眼睛;
我自己的痴爱使我辗转反侧,
为了你的缘故而整夜地打更。
　　我为你失眠, 而你在别处作乐,
　　离得我远远的, 而和别人亲热。

Sonnet 62

Sin of self–love possesseth all mine eye,
And all my soul, and all my every part;
And for this sin there is no remedy,
It is so grounded inward in my heart.
Methinks no face so gracious is as mine,
No shape so true, no truth of such account,
And for myself mine own worth do define,
As I all other in all worths surmount.
But when my glass shows me myself indeed,
Beated and chopped with tanned antiquity,
Mine own self–love quite contrary I read;
Self so self–loving were iniquity.
    'Tis thee (my self) that for myself I praise,
    Painting my age with beauty of thy days.

六二

一种顾影自怜的毛病迷住了
我的眼、我的心，我的每一部分，
这毛病是无法可以救药，
它是深深地在我的心里生根。
我觉得无人有我这样俊秀的脸，
这样完美的体形，无事比这更要紧。
我自己私下估量我自己的优点[45]，
我在各方面超过了所有的人。
可是揽镜自照我的真面目，
憔悴，生满皱纹，而且苍老，
我发现我的自鸣得意是错误，
爱这样的自己毋乃太荒谬。
　　你才是我自己，我赞美的是你，
　　把你的青春粉饰了我这一把年纪。

Sonnet 63

Against my love shall be as I am now,
With Time's injurious hand crushed and o'erworn;
When hours have drained his blood and filled his brow
With lines and wrinkles; when his youthful morn
Hath travelled on to age's steepy night,
And all those beauties whereof now he's king
Are vanishing, or vanished out of sight,
Stealing away the treasure of his spring:
For such a time do I now fortify
Against confounding age's cruel knife,
That he shall never cut from memory
My sweet love's beauty, thought my lover's life.
    His beauty shall in these black lines be seen,
    And they shall live, and he in them still green.

六三

预防我的爱人将来和我一样，
被时间的毒手压平磨损，
光阴耗干他的血液，在他脸上
布满皱纹；他的青春之晨
要步入老年的崎岖的黑夜，
他现在唯我独尊的一切的美，
就要逐渐地完全消灭，
偷偷地带走他青春的宝贝。
我现在着手防备这时间的到来，
我要抵抗老年的利剑之残酷无情，
它纵然能把吾爱的性命破坏，
不能毁灭他的美貌留下的名声。
　　他的美永留在一行行黑字中间，
　　诗垂不朽，他在诗中永久新鲜。

Sonnet 64

When I have seen by Time's fell hand defaced
The rich proud cost of outworn buried age;
When sometime lofty towers I see down rased,
And brass eternal slave to mortal rage;
When I have seen the hungry ocean gain
Advantage on the kingdom of the shore,
And the firm soil win of the wat'ry main,
Increasing store with loss, and loss with store;
When I have seen such interchange of state,
Or state itself confounded to decay,
Ruin hath taught me thus to ruminate:
That Time will come and take my love away.
    This thought is as a death, which cannot choose
    But weep to have that which it fears to lose.

六四

我看到年湮代远的豪华工程
被时间的毒手所毁却；
我看到当年的高楼被夷平，
永生的铜碑禁不起死神肆虐；
我看到饥饿贪食的沧海
吞没岸边陆地的良田，
陆地又把海的领域夺了回来，
互有盈亏地更番侵占；
我看到这样的荣辱无常，
繁华终究归于死寂，
这惨况使我不免要思量，
时间会把我的爱人夺去。
　　想到这里有如死别，不能不唏嘘，
　　因为我现在所有的终有丧失之虞。

Sonnet 65

Since brass, nor stone, nor earth, nor boundless sea,
But sad mortality o'ersways their power,
How with this rage shall beauty hold a plea,
Whose action is no stronger than a flower?
O how shall summer's honey breath hold out
Against the wrackful siege of batt'ring days,
When rocks impregnable are not so stout,
Nor gates of steel so strong, but Time decays?
O fearful meditation! Where, alack,
Shall Time's best jewel from Time's chest lie hid?
Or what strong hand can hold his swift foot back,
Or who his spoil of beauty can forbid?
O none, unless this miracle have might,
That in black ink my love may still shine bright.

六五

既然铜、石、陆地、无边的海洋
都抵不住死亡之毁灭的暴力，
美貌的活力不比一朵花儿强，
能有什么力量和暴力抗拒？
啊，夏季之一阵阵的花香，
如何禁得一天天的风狂雨暴？
岩石不够硬，钢门不够强，
都不免要被时间毁掉。
想来真是可怕！何处藏这天生的宝贝，
才可不被装进时间的宝箱？
何等的巨手才能扯回时间的快腿？
谁能制止它对美貌的劫掠？
　　没有人能，除非这个奇迹生效，
　　我的爱人在我的诗里永久照耀。

Sonnet 66

Tired with all these, for restful death I cry:
As to behold desert a beggar born,
And needy nothing trimmed in jollity,
And purest faith unhappily forsworn,
And gilded honour shamefully misplaced,
And maiden virtue rudely strumpeted,
And right perfection wrongfully disgraced,
And strength by limping sway disablèd,
And art made tongue–tied by authority,
And folly (doctor–like) controlling skill,
And simple truth miscalled simplicity,
And captive good attending captain ill:
    Tired with all these, from these would I be gone,
    Save that to die, I leave my love alone.

六六 [46]

这些我厌倦了，我要在死中安息，
例如看着天才生而为乞丐，
蠢货反倒穿戴得堂皇富丽；
最纯洁的誓约惨遭破坏，
金亮的荣誉被放错了地方；
处女的贞操被人横加污辱，
一代完人的名誉被人中伤；
懦者当权，强者徒呼负负，
学术慑于权势不敢发言，
愚昧假充内行对专家发号施令；
真诚被目为头脑简单，
良善服从邪恶的乱命。
　　这些我看厌了，我要离开这人世，
　　只是我若一死，我的爱人形单影只。

Sonnet 67

Ah wherefore with infection should he live,
And with his presence grace impiety,
That sin by him advantage should achieve,
And lace itself with his society?
Why should false painting imitate his cheek,
And steal dead seeing of his living hue?
Why should poor beauty indirectly seek
Roses of shadow, since his rose is true?
Why should he live, now Nature bankrout is,
Beggared of blood to blush through lively veins,
For she hath no exchequer now but his,
And proud of many, lives upon his gains?
　O him she stores, to show what wealth she had,
　In days long since, before these last so bad.

六七[47]

啊，为什么他活在这龌龊世界里，
为那些邪恶的人们增光，
以至于罪恶因他而讨到便宜，
有他做伴而得意扬扬？
为什么要用脂粉冒充他的容颜，
从他的生动的神采偷取死板的模样[48]？
他脸上既已具有玫瑰的鲜艳，
又何必摹绘那玫瑰的影像？
“自然”既已破产，脉管里缺乏血流，
无以滋润她的朱颜，他为什么还要独活？
因为她除了他的美貌已一无所有，
过去人才辈出，现在只靠他一个。
　　啊，她保藏他，表示许久以前
　　她何等富有，不似如今这等寒酸。

Sonnet 68

Thus is his cheek the map of days outworn,
When beauty lived and died as flowers do now,
Before these bastard signs of fair were borne,
Or durst inhabit on a living brow;
Before the golden tresses of the dead,
The right of sepulchres, were shorn away,
To live a second life on second head;
Ere beauty's dead fleece made another gay:
In him those holy àntique hours are seen,
Without all ornament, itself and true,
Making no summer of another's green,
Robbing no old to dress his beauty new;
    And him as for a map doth Nature store,
    To show false Art what beauty was of yore.

六八

他的脸是古往时代的象征，

美貌的盛衰有如花开花落，

那时候人造的脂粉尚未发明，

也不敢往活人的脸上涂抹；

那时候死人的金黄发鬈

是属于坟墓的，没人把它剪下来，

在别人头上再活一个第二遍，

死人的毛发不装潢活人的脑袋。

在他的脸上可以看到往昔盛世，

朴实无华，一向保持本来面目[49]，

不用别个的绿叶假充夏季，

不劫夺死者来装扮新的人物：

　　“自然”保藏他，像保藏图表一帧，

　　给擦胭抹粉的人看看古代的美人。

Sonnet 69

Those parts of thee that the world's eye doth view
Want nothing that the thought of hearts can mend;
All tongues (the voice of souls) give thee that due,
Utt'ring bare truth, even so as foes commend.
Thy outward thus with outward praise is crowned,
But those same tongues that give thee so thine own,
In other accents do this praise confound
By seeing farther than the eye hath shown.
They look into the beauty of thy mind,
And that in guess they measure by thy deeds;
Then, churls, their thoughts (although their eyes were kind)
To thy fair flower add the rank smell of weeds:
　　But why thy odour matcheth not thy show,
　　The soil is this, that thou dost common grow.

六九

你身上所共见的各个部分，
尽善尽美，怎样想也无以复加；
人人都衷心地对你加以承认，
说的是实情，恰似敌人之不肯过夸。
你的仪表受到了表面的赞扬，
但是这些极口赞美你的人们，
比用眼睛做更深一层的估量，
立刻改变语调，一反赞美的口吻。
他们要对你内心的美加以探讨，
以你的行为做估量的准绳。
蠢材们，虽然眼睛对你很好，
他们心中却给你的花容加上臭名。
　　何以你的气味和外表不能相称，
　　答案是——你是个随波逐流的人。

Sonnet 70

That thou are blamed shall not be thy defect,
For slander's mark was ever yet the fair;
The ornament of beauty is suspèct,
A crow that flies in heaven's sweetest air.
So thou be good, slander doth but approve
Thy worth the greater, being wooed of time,
For canker vice the sweetest buds doth love,
And thou present'st a pure unstainèd prime.
Thou hast passed by the ambush of young days,
Either not assailed, or victor being charged,
Yet this thy praise cannot be so thy praise
To tie up envy, evermore enlarged:
    If some suspèct of ill masked not thy show,
    Then thou alone kingdoms of hearts shouldst owe.

七〇

你受责备，这不是你的缺失，
因为流言总是以美貌做箭靶。
遭嫉乃是美貌的一项装饰，
有如晴空万里飞过一只乌鸦。
只消你洁身自好，毁谤只能证明
你的人品高，为大众所喜爱；
罪恶有如害虫钻入最香的蓓蕾之中，
而你正在天真无邪的青春时代，
你已经躲过青春时代的埋伏，
没受到诱惑，或已战胜了诱惑。
可是这赞美不能长久地缚住
那永无遮拦的嫉妒的口舌。
　　如果你的仪表没有蒙上恶意的猜忌，
　　你便是天下无双，万众归心于你。

Sonnet 71

No longer mourn for me when I am dead
Than you shall hear the surly sullen bell
Give warning to the world that I am fled
From this vile world with vildest worms to dwell;
Nay, if you read this line, remember not
The hand that writ it, for I love you so
That I in your sweet thoughts would be forgot,
If thinking on me then should make you woe.
O if (I say) you look upon this verse,
When I (perhaps) compounded am with clay,
Do not so much as my poor name rehearse,
But let your love even with my life decay,
    Lest the wise world should look into your moan,
    And mock you with me after I am gone.

七一

你听到丧钟沉重地响起，
通告世人我已经离开
这万恶世界去和蛆虫同居，
你就不要再为我而悲哀。
不，你若读到此诗，不要怀想
写诗的人，因为我爱你太深，
我情愿被人所遗忘，
如果想起我来你太伤心。
如果我已和泥土混在一起，
你偶然看到这首小诗，
请连我的名字都不必再提，
让你的爱和我的生命一起消逝。
　　否则世人要追问你忧伤的缘故，
　　使你在我死后和我一同受到侮辱。

Sonnet 72

O lest the world should task you to recite
What merit lived in me that you should love,
After my death (dear love) forget me quite;
For you in me can nothing worthy prove,
Unless you would devise some virtuous lie
To do more for me than mine own desert,
And hang more praise upon deceasèd I
Than niggard truth would willingly impart:
O lest your true love may seem false in this,
That you for love speak well of me untrue,
My name be buried where my body is,
And live no more to shame nor me nor you:
　For I am shamed by that which I bring forth,
　And so should you, to love things nothing worth.

七二

啊！我死后世人怕要逼你说
我有何德值得你爱，
所以，亲爱的，请完全忘了我，
我有什么好处你说不出来。
除非你肯捏造弥天大谎
来称颂我，超过我应得之份，
对我这死人大加揄扬，
超过真理之所甘愿承认。
啊！这样你的爱怕不像真诚的爱，
你是为了爱而称赞我，而作假，
所以我的名字该和我的身体一起埋，
不要再为你或为我招人笑骂。
　　因为我对我的作品感到羞惭[50]，
　　你竟垂爱，也会觉得有失体面。

Sonnet 73

That time of year thou mayst in me behold
When yellow leaves, or none, or few, do hang
Upon those boughs which shake against the cold,
Bare ruined choirs, where late the sweet birds sang.
In me thou seest the twilight of such day
As after sunset fadeth in the west,
Which by and by black night doth take away,
Death's second self, that seals up all in rest.
In me thou seest the glowing of such fire
That on the ashes of his youth doth lie,
As the death–bed whereon it must expire,
Consumed with that which it was nourished by.
  This thou perceiv'st, which makes thy love more strong,
  To love that well which thou must leave ere long.

七三

从我身上你可看到这样的季节，
寒风中抖颤着的树枝上面
是光秃秃的，或只挂着几片黄叶，
像是好鸟栖过的唱坛废墟一般；
从我身上你可看到这样的黄昏，
夕阳已经在西方褪了颜色，
不久黑夜那死亡的化身
就会把它取走，使一切安息静卧；
从我身上你可看到这样的火亮，
躺在青春的灰烬上面酣睡，
好像它必须命终在那死人床上，
被维持生命的东西把生命销毁。
　　你看到这些，你会爱得更深，
　　爱那你不久即将永别的人。

Sonnet 74

But be contented when that fell arrest
Without all bail shall carry me away,
My life hath in this line some interest,
Which for memorial still with thee shall stay.
When thou reviewest this, thou dost review
The very part was consecrate to thee:
The earth can have but earth, which is his due;
My spirit is thine, the better part of me.
So then thou hast but lost the dregs of life,
The prey of worms, my body being dead,
The coward conquest of a wretch's knife,
Too base of thee to be rememberèd:
    The worth of that is that which it contains,
    And that is this, and this with thee remains.

七四

但是我若被凶狠狠地拘捕而去，

并且没人来保释我，你大可放心。

我的生命有一部分存在这诗里，

它会长伴着你做永久的纪念品。

你重读这首诗，你就会再度看出

其中主要部分是献给了你的。

泥土只能收回它所应得的泥土，

我的较好部分，我的精神，属于你。

所以你损失的只是生命渣滓，

我的躯体死了只是蛆虫的食物，

凶汉刀下之怯懦的牺牲者[51]，

太低贱了，不值得令你回顾。

　　躯体的价值在于它含有精神，

　　那精神即是我的诗，诗将与你共存。

Sonnet 75

So are you to my thoughts as food to life,
Or as sweet seasoned showers are to the ground;
And for the peace of you I hold such strife
As 'twixt a miser and his wealth is found:
Now proud as an enjoyer, and anon
Doubting the filching age will steal his treasure;
Now counting best to be with you alone,
Then bettered that the world may see my pleasure:
Sometime all full with feasting on your sight,
And by and by clean starvèd for a look;
Possessing or pursuing no delight
Save what is had or must from you be took.
    Thus do I pine and surfeit day by day,
    Or gluttoning on all, or all away.

七五 [52]

你于我心犹如食物之于生命，
又如及时甘霖之于土地。
为享受你的友爱我心不宁，
像守财奴对于财富之忧虑，
时而以拥有多资而自傲，
又怕世人觊觎偷去他的宝藏；
时而以和你单独厮守为最好，
时而又想世人看看我的得意扬扬；
有时候我已饱餐了你的秀色，
不久又想看你，而且十分情急。
我不追求也不能有任何快乐，
除非那快乐是自你那里来的。
　　我就这样地一天挨饿一天饱撑，
　　不是尽情饕餮，便是席上空空。

Sonnet 76

Why is my verse so barren of new pride?
So far from variation or quick change?
Why with the time do I not glance aside
To new–found methods and to compounds strange?
Why write I still all one, ever the same,
And keep invention in a noted weed,
That every word doth almost tell my name,
Showing their birth, and where they did proceed?
O know, sweet love, I always write of you,
And you and love are still my argument;
So all my best is dressing old words new,
Spending again what is already spent:
    For as the sun is daily new and old,
    So is my love still telling what is told.

七六 [53]

我的诗何以这样缺乏新鲜花样，
这样缺乏变化或敏捷的才思？
我对时髦作风何不加以模仿，
使用新奇笔调或诡异的复合名词？
我为什么写法总是千篇一律，
有所创作总是穿着陈旧衣裳，
每个字几乎可以宣示我的名字，
露出身份以及来自何方？
你要知道，爱人，我写的永远是你，
你与爱永远是我的题材；
我擅长的是把旧词变成新的，
已经用过的不妨再用一回：

　　太阳每日出没，新旧递嬗，
　　我的爱也永远是老调重弹。

Sonnet 77

Thy glass will show thee how thy beauties wear,
Thy dial how thy precious minutes waste,
The vacant leaves thy mind's imprint will bear,
And of this book, this learning mayst thou taste:
The wrinkles which thy glass will truly show
Of mouthèd graves will give thee memory;
Thou by thy dial's shady stealth mayst know
Time's thievish progress to eternity;
Look what thy memory cannot contain
Commit to these waste blanks, and thou shalt find
Those children nursed, delivered from thy brain,
To take a new acquaintance of thy mind.
These offices, so oft as thou wilt look,
Shall profit thee, and much enrich thy book.

七七[54]

镜子将告诉你，你的美在逝去，
日晷将告诉你，你的时光在流转，
这些空页将负载你心思的痕迹，
从这册子你将尝到这样的指点[55]：
你的镜子正确映出的满脸皱褶
能使你记起那敞着大口的坟墓；
你从那日晷的阴影之偷偷摸摸
可知时间正向着永恒偷偷迈步。
凡是你的记忆收藏不下的事情
可以记在这空白页上，你会发现
从你脑中产生出来的那些儿童
养大之后会像你新认识的人一般。
　　你若常看这些事物所发生的作用[56]，
　　不仅你获益，并可充实这册子的内容。

Sonnet 78

So oft have I invoked thee for my Muse,
And found such fair assistance in my verse,
As every alien pen hath got my use,
And under thee their poesy disperse.
Thine eyes, that taught the dumb on high to sing,
And heavy ignorance aloft to fly,
Have added feathers to the learnèd's wing
And given grace a double majesty.
Yet be most proud of that which I compile,
Whose influence is thine, and born of thee:
In others' works thou dost but mend the style,
And arts with thy sweet graces gracèd be;
　But thou art all my art, and dost advance
　As high as learning my rude ignorance.

七八

我常常乞求你做我的诗神，
笔下果然获得很多的灵感，
于是每个文人都学我的窍门，
在你的眷顾之下发表诗篇。
你的眼睛曾教哑巴高声歌唱，
曾教笨重的冥顽翱翔于天空，
居然把羽毛加在学者的翅上[57]，
使得尊贵的人得到双倍威风。
请以我的作品为最值得骄傲，
那是受你的启发，那是你的产物。
在别人作品里你只是润饰笔调，
用你的威仪来装点他们的学术。
　　但你是我艺术的全部，你把我的愚顽
　　高高地抬举到和学者一般。

Sonnet 79

Whilst I alone did call upon thy aid,
My verse alone had all thy gentle grace,
But now my gracious numbers are decayed,
And my sick Muse doth give another place.
I grant (sweet love) thy lovely argument
Deserves the travail of a worthier pen,
Yet what of thee thy poet doth invent
He robs thee of, and pays it thee again:
He lends thee virtue, and he stole that word
From thy behaviour; beauty doth he give,
And found it in thy cheek; he can afford
No praise to thee but what in thee doth live.
    Then thank him not for that which he doth say,
    Since what he owes thee, thou thyself dost pay.

七九

我从前独自向你乞灵，

我的诗独得你全部的欢心；

如今我献媚的诗篇开始失宠，

我的拙作让位给另外一个人。

我承认，亲爱的，你这题材太美，

应由较健的手笔来处理。

不过你那诗人笔下尽管天花乱坠，

其实是从你身上抢来又送还给你的。

他说你有美德，那句话

是他窃自你的行为；他说你美，

那是他在你脸上发现的；

他夸你的种种，你早已就都具备。

　　那么为了他的话你无须感激，

　　因为他该给你的原是你自己付出去的。

Sonnet 80

O how I faint when I of you do write,
Knowing a better spirit doth use your name,
And in the praise thereof spends all his might,
To make me tongue–tied speaking of your fame.
But since your worth (wide as the ocean is)
The humble as the proudest sail doth bear,
My saucy bark (inferior far to his)
On your broad main doth wilfully appear.
Your shallowest help will hold me up afloat,
Whilst he upon your soundless deep doth ride,
Or (being wracked) I am a worthless boat,
He of tall building and of goodly pride.
    Then if he thrive and I be cast away,
    The worst was this: my love was my decay.

八〇

提笔写你的时候我好心灰意懒，
明知另有高才在使用你的名义，
他用尽全力对你加以称赞，
使我闭口结舌无从表扬你的令誉！
但是你的优点，浩如海洋，
负载扁舟一如负载巨舰，
我的小船远不如他的堂皇，
偏要在你的广阔海面出现。
你的浅滩就可以把我浮起，
他只能在你深不可测之处航行。
我即使触礁，破船损失无几，
他则高樯壮丽，损失不轻。
　　如果他成功而我被遗弃，
　　最恼的人是——我的爱使我一败涂地。

Sonnet 81

Or I shall live your epitaph to make,
Or you survive when I in earth am rotten,
From hence your memory death cannot take,
Although in me each part will be forgotten.
Your name from hence immortal life shall have,
Though I (once gone) to all the world must die;
The earth can yield me but a common grave,
When you intombèd in men's eyes shall lie:
Your monument shall be my gentle verse,
Which eyes not yet created shall o'er–read,
And tongues to be your being shall rehearse,
When all the breathers of this world are dead;
  You still shall live (such virtue hath my pen)
  Where breath most breathes, even in the mouths of men.

八一

不是我活着为你写墓铭，
便是你活着而我已变烂泥。
死神不能夺去你在世间的名声，
虽然我的每一特点都会被人忘记。
你的大名将永垂万古，
虽然我一死便默默无闻；
人间只能给我一抔黄土，
你将在众人眼里筑起高坟。
你的纪念碑便是我的温柔诗句，
未来的眼睛会加以吟诵。
等到现世的活人都已死去，
未来的舌头会谈论你的生平。
　　你将永生不朽——我的笔有这等魅力——
　　在有生人呼吸的地方，在众人的口里。

Sonnet 82

I grant thou wert not married to my Muse,
And therefore mayst without attaint o'erlook
The dedicated words which writers use
Of their fair subject, blessing every book.
Thou art as fair in knowledge as in hue,
Finding thy worth a limit past my praise,
And therefore art inforced to seek anew
Some fresher stamp of the time–bettering days.
And do so, love; yet when they have devised
What strainèd touches rhetoric can lend,
Thou, truly fair, wert truly sympathised
In true plain words by thy true–telling friend;
    And their gross painting might be better used
    Where cheeks need blood; in thee it is abused.

八二

我承认你没有和我的诗神结婚，
所以作家们对于他们的美丽题目
写些仰慕的词句讨你的欢心，
你可以逐册地披览，不算错误。
你的学识和丰采是一般地高超，
觉得我的赞美尚不足以表彰你，
于是你不得不到别处去寻找
当代较进步的较清新的手笔。
可以的，爱；不过他们文思驰骋，
不外是修辞上勉强的堆砌而已，
你是真正的美，你最忠实的反映
是在说实话的朋友之坦白陈述里；
　　他们的浓装艳抹的笔法不妨
　　用在贫血的脸上，对你是用错了地方。

Sonnet 83

I never saw that you did painting need,
And therefore to your fair no painting set;
I found (or thought I found) you did exceed
The barren tender of a poet's debt:
And therefore have I slept in your report,
That you yourself, being extant, well might show
How far a modern quill doth come too short,
Speaking of worth, what worth in you doth grow.
This silence for my sin you did impute,
Which shall be most my glory, being dumb,
For I impair not beauty, being mute,
When others would give life, and bring a tomb.
    There lives more life in one of your fair eyes
    Than both your poets can in praise devise.

八三

我从不觉得你需要粉饰，
所以我不为你的美貌装潢。
我觉得——自以为觉得——你胜似
一个诗人所能献给你的辞章，
所以我没有积极地颂扬你。
你自己在活着，即可充分证明
庸俗的鹅翎管如何地贫乏无力。
讲到才德，你是如何地头角峥嵘。
你以为这沉默是我的罪状，
其实哑口无言是我最光荣之处，
因为我保持沉默没有把美损伤，
别人想给你永生，却带来了坟墓。
　　你的一只亮晶晶的眼睛，
　　比两个诗人的谀辞更有生命[58]。

Sonnet 84

Who is it that says most which can say more
Than this rich praise - that you alone are you,
In whose confine immurèd is the store
Which should example where your equal grew?
Lean penury within that pen doth dwell
That to his subject lends not some small glory,
But he that writes of you, if he can tell
That you are you, so dignifies his story:
Let him but copy what in you is writ,
Not making worse what nature made so clear,
And such a counterpart shall fame his wit,
Making his style admirèd every where.
　You to your beauteous blessings add a curse,
　Being fond on praise, which makes your praises worse.

八四

谁说得最彻底[59]？哪个能说出
比这更丰富的赞词——“你就是你”？
在你的范围之内有了美的全部，
你只能提供你自己来和你匹敌。
那支秃笔实在是寒酸，
若不能给他的对象增光；
但是写你的人若能称赞
“你就是你”，这也就足够堂皇。
让他照抄你身上写着的文章，
不必损伤造物者的辉煌成绩，
这样的描绘可以使他文名大扬，
到处都会钦仰他的文笔。
　　你给你的美名带来了咒骂，
　　你太贪求赞美，反把赞美糟蹋。

Sonnet 85

My tongue–tied Muse in manners holds her still,
While comments of your praise, richly compiled,
Reserve their character with golden quill
And precious phrase by all the Muses filed.
I think good thoughts, whilst other write good words,
And like unlettered clerk still cry 'Amen'
To every hymn that able spirit affords
In polished form of well–refinèd pen.
Hearing you praised, I say, ''Tis so, 'tis true',
And to the most of praise add something more;
But that is in my thought, whose love to you
(Though words come hindmost) holds his rank before.
  Then others for the breath of words respect,
  Me for my dumb thoughts, speaking in effect.

八五

我的缄默的诗神礼貌地一声不作，
一般赞美你的作品却堂皇富丽，
为文字传诸久远，他们用金笔镂刻[60]，
所用辞藻是历代诗家琢磨过的。
别人的文字好，我的用心好，
我就像无学识的教堂小吏一般，
一俟每篇名家精撰的颂词唱完了，
我总是跟着喊出一声“阿门”。
听你受到赞美，我就说：“确是这样的。”
于他们的极口称赞之外我要加上一点，
不过这是我在心里想，这一番情意，
虽然说得最慢，实在是走在最前边。
　　那么对别人你要注意他们的文辞，
　　对我，注意我真诚而无言的表示。

Sonnet 86

Was it the proud full sail of his great verse,
Bound for the prize of all–too–precious you,
That did my ripe thoughts in my brain inhearse,
Making their tomb the womb wherein they grew?
Was it his spirit, by spirits taught to write
Above a mortal pitch, that struck me dead?
No, neither he, nor his compeers by night
Giving him aid, my verse astonishèd.
He, nor that affable familiar ghost
Which nightly gulls him with intelligence,
As victors, of my silence cannot boast;
I was not sick of any fear from thence;
    But when your countenance filled up his line,
    Then lacked I matter, that infeebled mine.

八六

是否他的伟大诗篇声势壮盛，
要前去掠劫你这个稀世之珍，
以致我的成熟思想在脑中葬送，
它们的胎腹变成了它们的坟？
是否他的心灵，得到精灵指点，
写得出神入化，给了我致命打击？
不，他，成半夜帮助他的那些伙伴[61]，
都不能把我的诗吓得麻痹。
他，或是以虚伪知识在夜间
来骗他的那位殷勤的精灵，
都不能夸说我被制得哑口无言，
我不是为怕他们而气馁心惊。

　　不过你的恩宠若注满了他的诗句，
　　我就没得可写，那就使我的作品空虚。

Sonnet 87

Farewell, thou art too dear for my possessing,
And like enough thou know’st thy estimate:
The charter of thy worth gives thee releasing;
My bonds in thee are all determinate.
For how do I hold thee but by thy granting,
And for that riches where is my deserving?
The cause of this fair gift in me is wanting,
And so my patent back again is swerving.
Thy self thou gav’st, thy own worth then not knowing,
Or me, to whom thou gav’st it, else mistaking;
So thy great gift, upon misprision growing,
Comes home again, on better judgement making.
  Thus have I had thee as a dream doth flatter,
  In sleep a king, but waking no such matter.

八七

再会！你太高贵，我配不上你，
也许是你认清了你自己的价值，
你这样高贵的身份有取舍的权利，
我对你的义务到此全部废止。
除非你准许，我怎能把你占有？
我又怎配享受那样一份财富？
我没有取得这份重礼的理由，
所以我的所有权又缴还原处。
你未认清自己的价值，故倾心相爱。
也许你倾心于我，是看错了人，
所以你的伟大礼物是由于误会，
审慎考虑之后又返回了家门。
　　我和你交欢有如一梦，
　　梦中为王，醒后一场空。

Sonnet 88

When thou shalt be disposed to set me light,
And place my merit in the eye of scorn,
Upon thy side against myself I'll fight,
And prove thee virtuous, though thou art forsworn:
With mine own weakness being best acquainted,
Upon thy part I can set down a story
Of faults concealed wherein I am attainted,
That thou in losing me shall win much glory;
And I by this will be a gainer too,
For, bending all my loving thoughts on thee,
The injuries that to myself I do,
Doing thee vantage, double vantage me.
    Such is my love, to thee I so belong,
    That for thy right myself will bear all wrong.

八八

有一天你若是看我不起，
使我在人眼前受到轻侮，
我要站在你那一面打击我自己，
证明你虽不够交情，却无错误。
我最明了我自己的弱点，
为支持你我可以自行摊牌，
和盘托出我的秘密缺陷。
你断绝我可以获得更多光彩，
我这样做也并不吃亏，
因为我全心全意地爱你。
我对我自己如此地诋毁，
于你有益，对我也就大大有利。
　　我的爱如此之深，我和你如此难舍难分，
　　为了你好，一切苦恼我都能忍。

Sonnet 89

Say that thou didst forsake me for some fault,
And I will comment upon that offence;
Speak of my lameness, and I straight will halt,
Against thy reasons making no defence.
Thou canst not (love) disgrace me half so ill,
To set a form upon desirèd change,
As I'll myself disgrace, knowing thy will:
I will acquaintance strangle and look strange,
Be absent from thy walks, and in my tongue
Thy sweet belovèd name no more shall dwell,
Lest I (too much profane) should do it wrong,
And haply of our old acquaintance tell.
For thee, against myself I'll vow debate,
For I must ne'er love him whom thou dost hate.

八九

若说因为我犯错才和我断绝，
我愿把那错误立即加以申说；
若说我跛脚，我立刻一拐一瘸，
你提出的理由我决不辩驳。
爱人，你表示愿意和我绝断，
这使我难堪，但是还赶不上
我先意承志自行贬抑之难堪的一半[62]：
此后我要和你断绝，做陌生人状，
躲避你常走动的地方，在我舌端
不再有你那亲密可爱的姓名，
怕的是渎亵过分，竟一时失检，
谈起我们以前交往的情形。
　　为了你，我发誓要对自我宣战，
　　因为你所恨的人我决不留恋。

Sonnet 90

Then hate me when thou wilt, if ever, now,
Now while the world is bent my deeds to cross,
Join with the spite of Fortune, make me bow,
And do not drop in for an after–loss.
Ah do not, when my heart hath scaped this sorrow,
Come in the rearward of a conquered woe;
Give not a windy night a rainy morrow,
To linger out a purposed overthrow.
If thou wilt leave me, do not leave me last,
When other petty griefs have done their spite,
But in the onset come; so shall I taste
At first the very worst of Fortune's might;
    And other strains of woe, which now seem woe,
    Compared with loss of thee, will not seem so.

九〇

想恨我就恨我吧。要恨，现在就恨。
现在，趁世人都在想打击我，
和命运之神联起手来使我俯首受困，
不要等到以后突然给我折磨。
啊！不要等到我的心已逃出这场苦恼，
在已被克服的悲哀之后又来反扑。
一夜风狂，不可再有清晨的雨暴，
延长我的不可避免的苦楚。
你若想离我而去，别最后再走，
别等其他伤心小事先把我熬炼，
参加第一批攻势吧，以便一开头
我就尝到命运之最恶劣的手段。
　　忧伤万缕，现在看来都像是忧伤，
　　若和失掉你一比，怕就要不像。

Sonnet 91

Some glory in their birth, some in their skill,
Some in their wealth, some in their body's force,
Some in their garments, though new–fangled ill,
Some in their hawks and hounds, some in their horse;
And every humour hath his adjunct pleasure,
Wherein it finds a joy above the rest;
But these particulars are not my measure:
All these I better in one general best.
Thy love is better than high birth to me,
Richer than wealth, prouder than garments' cost,
Of more delight than hawks or horses be;
And having thee, of all men's pride I boast:
  Wretched in this alone, that thou mayst take
  All this away, and me most wretched make.

九一

有些人夸耀门阀，有些人夸耀才学高；
有些人夸耀财富，有些人夸耀体力；
有些人夸耀服装，虽然是可厌的时髦；
有些人夸耀鹰犬，有些人夸耀马匹。
各种性格自有其附属的快乐，
各在其中得到无上的乐趣。
但是这些东西不能满足我，
我有一项快乐胜过这一切东西。
你的爱胜过你的高贵门阀，
比财富更丰盛，比服装更高贵，
比鹰和马更好耍。
有了你，我有了一切人的宝贝。
　　唯一遗憾的是，怕有一天
　　你拿走这一切，使得我极度寒酸。

Sonnet 92

But do thy worst to steal thyself away,
For term of life thou art assurèd mine,
And life no longer than thy love will stay,
For it depends upon that love of thine.
Then need I not to fear the worst of wrongs,
When in the least of them my life hath end;
I see a better state to me belongs
Than that which on thy humour doth depend.
Thou canst not vex me with inconstant mind,
Since that my life on thy revolt doth lie.
O what a happy title do I find,
Happy to have thy love, happy to die!
  But what's so blessèd–fair that fears no blot?
  Thou mayst be false, and yet I know it not.

九二

但是你尽可施展绝招，偷偷地溜走，
因为终我一生你都是属于我的。
我的生命不能比你的爱滞留更久，
因为它是靠了你的爱才能延续。
我无须恐惧遭受最严重的打击[63]，
你稍有冷漠的表示我就会命终。
我以为死是一个较佳的境遇，
胜似观察你的颜色而苟且偷生。
你三心二意不能使我烦恼，
因为你变心就会置我于死地。
啊，何等荣幸的权利令我获得了，
荣幸地获得你的爱，荣幸地死去！
　　什么美妙的事物没有污损之虞？
　　也许你已变心而我尚无所悉。

Sonnet 93

So shall I live, supposing thou art true,
Like a deceivèd husband; so love's face
May still seem love to me, though altered new;
Thy looks with me, thy heart in other place:
For there can live no hatred in thine eye,
Therefore in that I cannot know thy change.
In many's looks, the false heart's history
Is writ in moods and frowns and wrinkles strange,
But heaven in thy creation did decree
That in thy face sweet love should ever dwell;
What e'er thy thoughts or thy heart's workings be,
Thy looks should nothing thence but sweetness tell.
  How like Eve's apple doth thy beauty grow,
  If thy sweet virtue answer not thy show!

九三

这样我还可活下去，误以你为忠贞，
像一个被骗的丈夫；爱情在表面上
还可像是爱情，虽然你是变了心；
你的脸对着我，你的心在别的地方，
你的脸上不可能存有厌恶，
所以在那里我无法觉察你变心。
许多人变了心，心事就会流露，
发脾气，锁眉头，满面冷漠的皱纹，
但是上天创造你的时候，
规定你的脸上永久存着爱，
不论有什么心事，起什么念头，
你的脸上只露出可喜的神态。
　　你的美貌多么像是夏娃的苹果，
　　如果你的外表不配合你的美德！

Sonnet 94

They that have pow'r to hurt, and will do none,
That do not do the thing they most do show,
Who, moving others, are themselves as stone,
Unmovèd, cold, and to temptation slow –
They rightly do inherit heaven's graces,
And husband nature's riches from expense;
They are the lords and owners of their faces,
Others but stewards of their excellence.
The summer's flow'r is to the summer sweet,
Though to itself it only live and die,
But if that flow'r with base infection meet,
The basest weed outbraves his dignity:
For sweetest things turn sourest by their deeds;
Lilies that fester smell far worse than weeds.

九四

有些人有伤人的力量而不想伤人，
好像要做一种事而并未去做，
能打动别人而自己如石一般坚贞，
稳定，冷峻，不易受人诱惑，
这样的人真是得到了上天的恩宠，
一点也不浪费自然赋予的资产。
他们是自己的面貌的主人公，
别人不过是他们的才貌的办事员。
夏日的花儿供夏日的观览，
它本身却只是花开花谢，
但那花儿若是遭恶疾感染，
最贱的莠草也比它漂亮一些。
　　因为最香的东西变得最臭，若是行为腐败，
　　烂的白百合花比莠草的味道更坏。

Sonnet 95

How sweet and lovely dost thou make the shame
Which, like a canker in the fragrant rose,
Doth spot the beauty of thy budding name!
O in what sweets dost thou thy sins inclose!
That tongue that tells the story of thy days
(Making lascivious comments on thy sport)
Cannot dispraise, but in a kind of praise,
Naming thy name, blesses an ill report.
O what a mansion have those vices got
Which for their habitation chose out thee,
Where beauty's veil doth cover every blot,
And all things turns to fair that eyes can see!
Take heed (dear heart) of this large privilege:
The hardest knife ill used doth lose his edge.

九五

你把耻辱装点得多么可喜，
像芬芳蔷薇中的一只蛀虫，
污染了你的含苞待放的美誉！
啊！你用何等香料掩饰你的罪行！
你说起你的日常生涯，
把你的拈花惹草说得淋漓尽致，
那不是自谴，而是一种自夸。
提你的姓名，就把恶行变成好事。
啊！那些罪恶有多么好的大厦一间，
它们要个住处竟选中了你。
美的面幕遮蔽了每个污点，
外表上的一切都成了美的！
　　使用这广泛特权，亲爱的，你要谨慎；
　　最锐利的刀，不善用就会丧失锋刃。

Sonnet 96

Some say thy fault is youth, some wantonness,
Some say thy grace is youth and gentle sport;
Both grace and faults are loved of more and less:
Thou mak'st faults graces that to thee resort.
As on the finger of a thronèd queen
The basest jewel will be well esteemed,
So are those errors that in thee are seen
To truths translated, and for true things deemed.
How many lambs might the stern wolf betray,
If like a lamb he could his looks translate!
How many gazers mightst thou lead away,
If thou wouldst use the strength of all thy state!
  But do not so; I love thee in such sort,
  As thou being mine, mine is thy good report.

九六

有人说你的缺点是年轻、荒唐，
有人说你的优点是年轻、浪漫，
缺点优点，贵贱都一样地欣赏。
缺点到你身上，你会变成优点。
若是戴上了王后娘娘的手指，
最贱的宝石也会受人的敬慕。
所以你身上若发现一些过失，
也会变成德行，被视为无误。
多少只羊要被恶狼欺侮，
如果他能变得和羊一样！
多少仰慕你的人要被你引入歧途，
如果你使出一切风流的力量！
　　但不可如此。我深深地爱着你，
　　你是我的，你的名誉也是我的[64]。

Sonnet 97

How like a winter hath my absence been
From thee, the pleasure of the fleeting year!
What freezings have I felt, what dark days seen!
What old December's bareness every where!
And yet this time removed was summer's time,
The teeming autumn big with rich increase,
Bearing the wanton burthen of the prime,
Like widowed wombs after their lords' decease:
Yet this abundant issue seem'd to me
But hope of orphans, and unfathered fruit,
For summer and his pleasures wait on thee,
And thou away, the very birds are mute;
Or if they sing, 'tis with so dull a cheer
That leaves look pale, dreading the winter's near.

九七

与君别离后，多像是过冬天，
你是时光流转中唯一的欢乐！
我觉得好冷，日子好黑暗！
好一派岁暮荒寒的景色！
这离别其实是在夏天[65]，
凸了肚皮的丰盛的秋季
承受着春天纵乐的负担，
像丈夫死后遗在腹内的子息。
不过对于我，这子孙的繁衍
只是生一个无父孤儿的指望。
因为夏天的欢乐都在你的身畔，
你一去，鸟儿都停了歌唱。
　　即使歌唱，也是无精打采，
　　使得树叶变色，生怕冬天要来。

Sonnet 98

From you have I been absent in the spring,
When proud–pied April (dressed in all his trim)
Hath put a spirit of youth in every thing,
That heavy Saturn laughed and leapt with him.
Yet nor the lays of birds, nor the sweet smell
Of different flowers in odour and in hue,
Could make me any summer's story tell,
Or from their proud lap pluck them where they grew:
Nor did I wonder at the lily's white,
Nor praise the deep vermilion in the rose;
They were but sweet, but figures of delight,
Drawn after you, you pattern of all those.
    Yet seemed it winter still, and, you away,
    As with your shadow I with these did play.

九八

我在春天离开了你，

那时骄艳的四月正在盛妆，

给一切注入了青春气息，

阴沉的土星都笑着和他跳荡[66]。

但是鸟啭和各种色香的花

所发散出来的芬芳气味，

都不能令我说开心的话，

或把花儿从花圃中摘了下来。

我不羡慕百合花的白，

也不赞美蔷薇花的红，

他们只是香，只是善于描摹

你这无美不臻的标准模型。

　　不过这依然像冬天。你不在身边，

　　我赏花，就像是和你的影子玩。

Sonnet 99

The forward violet thus did I chide:
'Sweet thief, whence didst thou steal thy sweet that smells,
If not from my love's breath? The purple pride
Which on thy soft cheek for complexion dwells
In my love's veins thou hast too grossly dyed.'
The lily I condemnèd for thy hand,
And buds of marjoram had stol'n thy hair;
The roses fearfully on thorns did stand,
One blushing shame, another white despair;
A third, nor red nor white, had stol'n of both,
And to his robb'ry had annexed thy breath,
But for his theft in pride of all his growth
A vengeful canker eat him up to death.
More flowers I noted, yet I none could see
But sweet or colour it had stol'n from thee.

九九[67]

我这样谴责那早开的紫罗兰:
艳贼,若非取自我爱人的呼气,
你那香味哪里偷来的?你那嫩脸
偷得一层红润,堂皇而富丽,
必是你大胆染自我爱人的血管。
我斥责百合偷你手上白皙的颜色,
薄荷花苞偷了你的头发香。
蔷薇在刺枝上惶悚地挂着,
红的是羞愧,白的是慌张,
不红不白的是两者各偷了一点[68],
颜色之外还加上了你的吐气香。
但是为了偷窃,乘他正在成熟发展,
一只报复的蛀虫把他吃得精光。
　　我看过很多花,但尚未见过一朵
　　其色香不是从你身上偷得。

Sonnet 100

Where art thou, Muse, that thou forget'st so long
To speak of that which gives thee all thy might?
Spend'st thou thy fury on some worthless song,
Dark'ning thy pow'r to lend base subjects light?
Return, forgetful Muse, and straight redeem
In gentle numbers time so idly spent;
Sing to the ear that doth thy lays esteem,
And gives thy pen both skill and argument.
Rise, resty Muse, my love's sweet face survey,
If Time have any wrinkle graven there;
If any, be a satire to decay,
And make Time's spoils despisèd every where.
    Give my love fame faster than Time wastes life;
    So thou prevent'st his scythe and crookèd knife.

一〇〇[69]

你在哪里，诗神，你这样久忘了
谈谈那启发你全部力量的话题？
你的灵感全在无聊诗篇里消耗掉，
贬损你的力量去光耀低级的东西？
回来吧，健忘的诗神，立刻去用
高尚的诗歌赎回这样浪费的时光。
唱给尊重你的作品的人听，
向使你获得诗意的人去歌唱。
起来，懒的诗神，看看我的爱人的面孔，
“时间”有无刻下一些皱纹在那里，
如果有，你要对那毁灭力量加以讥讽，
令“时间”的暴行到处被人看不起。
　　给我的爱人扬名，要快过消耗生命的时间，
　　你便可抢在他的镰刀和凶器之先。

Sonnet 101

O truant Muse, what shall be thy amends
For thy neglect of truth in beauty dyed?
Both truth and beauty on my love depends;
So dost thou too, and therein dignified.
Make answer, Muse, wilt thou not haply say,
'Truth needs no colour with his colour fixed,
Beauty no pencil, beauty's truth to lay;
But best is best, if never intermixed'?
Because he needs no praise, wilt thou be dumb?
Excuse not silence so, for't lies in thee
To make him much outlive a gilded tomb,
And to be praised of ages yet to be.
Then do thy office, Muse; I teach thee how
To make him seem long hence as he shows now.

一〇一

玩忽的诗神哪，你怠慢了
美貌的真诚，其将何以补偿？
真与美都以我的爱人为依靠[70]：
你也是一样，靠他才显得辉煌。
回答，诗神，也许你要说：
“真的本色不需要再润饰一下，
美不需要画笔再来涂抹，
最好的永远是最好的，何必羼假？”
只因他不需要赞美，你就噤不作声？
不要这样为沉默辩解，因为你有能力
使他能有比一座金坟更垂久远的美名，
使他受未来一代一代的赞誉。
　　那么执行任务吧，诗神，我教你怎样
　　使他以后长和现在一般地漂亮。

Sonnet 102

My love is strength'ned, though more weak in seeming;
I love not less, though less the show appear:
That love is merchandised whose rich esteeming
The owner's tongue doth publish every where.
Our love was new, and then but in the spring,
When I was wont to greet it with my lays,
As Philomel in summer's front doth sing,
And stops his pipe in growth of riper days:
Not that the summer is less pleasant now
Than when her mournful hymns did hush the night,
But that wild music burthens every bough,
And sweets grown common lose their dear delight.
Therefore like her, I sometime hold my tongue,
Because I would not dull you with my song.

一〇二

我的爱心加强，虽然像是减弱；
我的爱没有减，虽然较少表现。
那种爱实乃普通的商货，
由货主到处宣扬它的优点。
我们当年初恋，情爱方萌，
我是常写诗篇吟咏我们的风流。
像夜莺在初夏新试歌声[71]，
到了夏杪就住了她的歌喉，
并非是夏季风光如今减了色，
不若她当初哀歌使得长夜屏息，
而是众鸟喧啾压得枝头欲堕，
美的东西变成庸俗就没有趣。
　　所以像夜莺一般我把口缄，
　　因我不愿以我的歌讨你的嫌。

Sonnet 103

Alack, what poverty my Muse brings forth,
That, having such a scope to show her pride,
The argument all bare is of more worth
Than when it hath my added praise beside.
O blame me not if I no more can write!
Look in your glass, and there appears a face
That overgoes my blunt invention quite,
Dulling my lines, and doing me disgrace.
Were it not sinful then, striving to mend,
To mar the subject that before was well?
For to no other pass my verses tend
Than of your graces and your gifts to tell;
　And more, much more than in my verse can sit,
　Your own glass shows you, when you look in it.

一〇三

哎呀，我的诗神带来的东西好寒碜，
有这样施展手段的好机会，
赤裸的题材居然大有可观，
比加上我一番赞美之后更美！
啊，莫怪我不能更赞一词！
照照镜子，就会看到一张脸，
比我的拙作更为楚楚有致，
使我的描写相形见绌，使我羞惭。
原来很好的素材，愈描愈糟，
那岂不是一桩罪过？
因为我的诗没有其他目标，
只想把你的才貌说一说：
　　你揽镜自照，你便有所得，
　　比我的诗所表现的要多得多。

Sonnet 104

To me, fair friend, you never can be old,
For as you were when first your eye I eyed,
Such seems your beauty still. Three winters cold
Have from the forests shook three summers's pride,
Three beauteous springs to yellow autumn turned
In process of the seasons have I seen,
Three April perfumes in three hot Junes burned,
Since first I saw you fresh which yet are green.
Ah yet doth beauty, like a dial hand,
Steal from his figure, and no pace perceived;
So your sweet hue, which methinks still doth stand,
Hath motion, and mine eye may be deceived;
    For fear of which, hear this, thou age unbred:
    Ere you were born was beauty's summer dead.

一〇四[72]

好朋友，你对我永远不会老，
因为当年我和你初次相逢，
到如今风采依旧：三度冬季寒飙，
吹落了林中三度夏季的盛容，
岁序转移之际我已经见过
三度美好春天变成黄色秋天，
自我初见你至今不变的颜色，
三度四月的香在热的六月里烧燃[73]。
美貌像是日晷上的时针一般
偷偷地走，瞧不出脚步移动，
你的风采亦如是，我以为永久不变，
其实是在动，是我的眼受了欺蒙。
　　因为有此一虑，未来的人请听我说：
　　你们未生之时，美的全盛时代已过。

Sonnet 105

Let not my love be called idolatry,
Nor my belovèd as an idol show,
Since all alike my songs and praises be
To one, of one, still such, and ever so.
Kind is my love today, tomorrow kind,
Still constant in a wondrous excellence;
Therefore my verse, to constancy confined,
One thing expressing, leaves out difference.
'Fair, kind, and true' is all my argument,
'Fair, kind, and true', varying to other words,
And in this change is my invention spent,
Three themes in one, which wondrous scope affords.
'Fair', 'kind', and 'true' have often lived alone,
Which three till now never kept seat in one.

一〇五

莫把我的爱情唤作偶像崇拜，
也莫把我的爱人当作偶像，
只因我的诗歌和赞美都一概[74]
献给一个人，千篇一律，永不变样。
我的爱人今日温柔，明日温柔，
那美好的心肠永久不变。
所以我的诗歌颂扬你的敦厚，
只表达一种心情，没有改换。
“美貌、温柔、忠实”是我全部主题，
“美貌、温柔、忠实”万变不离其宗。
在这变化之中我用尽我的想象力，
一个题目包含三个，题材自然无穷。
　　美貌、温柔、忠实，常是孤立无邻，
　　在此以前从不永久荟萃于一身。

Sonnet 106

When in the chronicle of wasted time
I see descriptions of the fairest wights,
And beauty making beautiful old rhyme
In praise of ladies dead and lovely knights,
Then in the blazon of sweet beauty's best,
Of hand, of foot, of lip, of eye, of brow,
I see their àntique pen would have expressed
Even such a beauty as you master now.
So all their praises are but prophecies
Of this our time, all you prefiguring,
And for they looked but with divining eyes
They had not skill enough your worth to sing:
For we, which now behold these present days,
Have eyes to wonder, but lack tongues to praise.

一〇六

我在过去的史纪当中，
看到最漂亮的人物的描述，
还有美人为古诗平添光荣，
赞美着古往的淑女和风流武士。
他们肆力描写美人最美的地方，
手、脚、嘴唇、眼睛、眉毛，
我就看出他们笔下是想
描绘出你现在所有的美貌。
所以他们的赞美不过是预言
我们这个时代，预报你的到来。
他们只是揣测一番，
无法颂扬你整个价值的所在[75]。
　　至于我们，生在当前这个时代之中，
　　只能瞪眼仰慕，不会张口赞颂。

Sonnet 107

Not mine own fears, nor the prophetic soul
Of the wide world, dreaming on things to come,
Can yet the lease of my true love control,
Supposed as forfeit to a confined doom.
The mortal moon hath her eclipse endured,
And the sad augurs mock their own presàge,
Incertainties now crown themselves assured,
And peace proclaims olives of endless age.
Now with the drops of this most balmy time
My love looks fresh, and Death to me subscribes,
Since spite of him I'll live in this poor rhyme,
While he insults o'er dull and speechless tribes.
  And thou in this shalt find thy monument,
  When tyrants' crests and tombs of brass are spent.

一〇七

我自己的疑虑，以及世人
对未来事物的臆料，
都还不能限制我相爱的真心，
不能认为期满而判为无效。
人间的明月安然度过了她的晦蚀[76]，
严肃的卜者嘲笑他们自己的预言，
动乱无常一变而为安若磐石，
和平宣告橄榄枝将流传万年。
受了这太平盛世雨露的沾润，
我的爱愈发鲜明。死神向我投降，
因为我不怕他，我在拙诗里长久生存，
他只能对愚昧无言的群众猖狂。
　　你在这诗里将扬名于永久，
　　帝王的勋饰与铜棺不免于腐朽。

Sonnet 108

What's in the brain that ink may character
Which hath not figured to thee my true spirit?
What's new to speak, what now to register,
That may express my love, or thy dear merit?
Nothing, sweet boy; but yet, like prayers divine,
I must each day say o'er the very same,
Counting no old thing old, thou mine, I thine,
Even as when first I hallowèd thy fair name.
So that eternal love in love's fresh case
Weighs not the dust and injury of age,
Nor gives to necessary wrinkles place,
But makes antiquity for aye his page,
    Finding the first conceit of love there bred,
    Where time and outward form would show it dead.

一〇八

脑子里有什么可以形诸笔墨的东西
而没有向你表达我的忠贞精神?
有什么新的可说，有什么可记载的，
来表示我的爱或你的优美的身份?
没有，亲爱的孩子。但是像对神祈祷，
我必须每天把同样的话再说一遍。
你是我的，我是你的，老调不嫌其老，
俨如我初次献诗给你的时候一般。
因此永恒的爱便可万古长新，
不介意人世的尘劳和岁月的伤害，
也不屈服于那无可避免的皱纹，
而把老年永远当作童仆看待[77]，
　　时间与外表宣告爱将死亡之际，
　　最初相恋的热情又复重新燃起。

Sonnet 109

O never say that I was false of heart,
Though absence seemed my flame to qualify;
As easy might I from my self depart
As from my soul, which in thy breast doth lie:
That is my home of love. If I have ranged,
Like him that travels I return again,
Just to the time, not with the time exchanged,
So that myself bring water for my stain.
Never believe, though in my nature reigned
All frailties that besiege all kinds of blood,
That it could so preposterously be stained
To leave for nothing all thy sum of good;
　For nothing this wide universe I call,
　Save thou, my rose; in it thou art my all.

一〇九[78]

啊！永勿说我用情不专，
虽然离别好像冷却了我的热情。
离开灵魂和离开本性是一样难，
我的灵魂是在你的胸膛之中，
那是我爱情的家；如果我放荡，
我已返回家门，像游子一般，
准时归来，没有因别离而变样，
这样我自己洗刷了我的污点。
即使我的内心深处
拥有各种情欲的弱点，
永毋相信我会荒唐到那种地步，
为不值一文的东西而把你弃捐。
　　我以为这广大世界都不值一顾，
　　除了你，我的蔷薇，你是我所有的全部。

Sonnet 110

Alas 'tis true, I have gone here and there,
And made myself a motley to the view,
Gored mine own thoughts, sold cheap what is most dear,
Made old offences of affections new.
Most true it is that I have looked on truth
Askance and strangely; but, by all above,
These blenches gave my heart another youth,
And worse essays proved thee my best of love.
Now all is done, have what shall have no end:
Mine appetite I never more will grind
On newer proof, to try an older friend,
A god in love, to whom I am confined.
    Then give me welcome, next my heaven the best,
    Even to thy pure and most most loving breast.

一一〇

哎呀，我确曾到处走来走去，
使我自己成了斑衣小丑[79]，
伤了自尊，廉售了最贵重的东西，
对新交出了旧的纰漏[80]。
的确我对忠实情感不曾正眼相看，
视若路人。但是，对天赌咒，
这样藐视使我的热情再度炽燃，
泛泛之交证明你才是我的挚友。
如今一切过去了，接受我永恒的爱。
我不再在新人身上磨砺我的感情，
以测验一个老朋友的价值之所在，
我只爱你，我只奉你为神明。
　　欢迎我吧，仅次于迎我进入天国去，
　　欢迎我进入你那纯洁可爱的胸怀里。

Sonnet 111

O for my sake do you with Fortune chide,
The guilty goddess of my harmful deeds,
That did not better for my life provide
Than public means which public manners breeds.
Thence comes it that my name receives a brand,
And almost thence my nature is subdued
To what it works in, like the dyer's hand.
Pity me then, and wish I were renewed,
Whilst like a willing patient I will drink
Potions of eisel 'gainst my strong infection;
No bitterness that I will bitter think,
Nor double penance to correct correction.
    Pity me then, dear friend, and I assure ye
    Even that your pity is enough to cure me.

———

啊！你要为我骂那命运女神，
是她使得我做下了丑事多端，
她没有为我准备较佳的福分，
我只得牺牲色相讨大众的喜欢，
于是烙印打在我的姓名之上，
我的本性几乎感染了
工作环境的色彩，像染工的手一样。
怜悯我吧，但愿我能洁身自好，
像一个病人似的我情愿吞服
一剂酸醋来治疗我的大症，
多苦的药我也不嫌其苦，
甘受双倍苦行做双倍的膺惩。
　　怜悯我吧，好朋友，我向你担保，
　　你的怜悯心就可以把我治好。

Sonnet 112

Your love and pity doth th'impression fill
Which vulgar scandal stamped upon my brow,
For what care I who calls me well or ill,
So you o'er–green my bad, my good allow?
You are my all the world, and I must strive
To know my shames and praises from your tongue;
None else to me, nor I to none alive,
That my steeled sense or changes right or wrong.
In so profound abysm I throw all care
Of others' voices, that my adder's sense
To critic and to flatterer stoppèd are.
Mark how with my neglect I do dispense:
    You are so strongly in my purpose bred
    That all the world besides methinks are dead.

一一二

你的爱与怜把人间的闲话
在我额上烙的疤痕给填平了，
别人说我好或坏，我何必管它，
只消你肯遮盖我的坏，承认我的好？
你是我整个世界，我要从你口中
知道我的耻辱与体面。
别人与我无关，谁也不能改动[81]
我之坚定的错误或正确的意见。
别人的意见我毫不关心，
一齐丢入深渊，对于诽谤与奉承，
我像蛇似的一概充耳不闻[82]。
看我怎样解释我的冷漠心情：
　　你如此根深蒂固地生在我心里，
　　我认为整个世界都已经死去[83]。

Sonnet 113

Since I left you, mine eye is in my mind,
And that which governs me to go about
Doth part his function, and is partly blind,
Seems seeing, but effectually is out;
For it no form delivers to the heart
Of bird, of flow'r, or shape which it doth latch;
Of his quick objects hath the mind no part;
Nor his own vision holds what it doth catch:
For if it see the rud'st or gentlest sight,
The most sweet favour or deformèd'st creature,
The mountain, or the sea, the day, or night,
The crow, or dove, it shapes them to your feature.
　　Incapable of more, replete with you,
　　My most true mind thus maketh mine eye untrue.

一一三

自从离开你，我的眼是在我心里，
至于指引我走路的那个器官，
只有部分机能，部分变成了瞎的[84]，
好像是能看，什么也看不见：
因为它看到了花鸟的形状，
不能把形状向我心里输送；
心不能分享眼中短暂的印象，
眼也不能保持那瞬间的幻影；
因为它看到的东西不拘粗或雅，
最美丽的容颜，最畸形的丑怪，
山或海，昼或夜，白鸽或乌鸦，
它把它们都变成了你的姿态。
　　心里全是你，不能承受别的东西，
　　我的忠心造成了我眼前的迷离[85]。

Sonnet 114

Or whether doth my mind being crowned with you
Drink up the monarch's plague, this flattery?
Or whether shall I say mine eye saith true,
And that your love taught it this alcumy,
To make of monsters, and things indigest,
Such cherubins as your sweet self resemble,
Creating every bad a perfect best
As fast as objects to his beams assemble?
O 'tis the first, 'tis flatt'ry in my seeing,
And my great mind most kingly drinks it up;
Mine eye well knows what with his gust is greeing,
And to his palate doth prepare the cup.
    If it be poisoned, 'tis the lesser sin
    That mine eye loves it and doth first begin.

一一四

究竟是我的心，有了你就自以为王，
吞下了帝王的毒药，这狂妄的自负？
还是我该说我的眼睛并未说诳，
是我对你的爱教它这套炼金术，
把妖怪畸形的东西
变成天使和你的模样相同，
每一件坏的都造得无懈可击，
眼的光芒所及立即迅速形成[86]？
啊！是前者，是我的看法狂妄，
我的骄纵的心竟一口把它吞掉。
我的眼深知它的口味怎样，
迎合它的口味调制这杯饮料。
　　如果其中有毒，罪也比较不大，
　　我的眼也爱它，自己先行喝下。

Sonnet 115

Those lines that I before have writ do lie,
Even those that said I could not love you dearer;
Yet then my judgement knew no reason why
My most full flame should afterwards burn clearer.
But reckoning Time, whose millioned accidents
Creep in 'twixt vows, and change decrees of kings,
Tan sacred beauty, blunt the sharp'st intents,
Divert strong minds to th'course of alt'ring things –
Alas, why, fearing of Time's tyranny,
Might I not then say 'Now I love you best',
When I was certain o'er incertainty,
Crowning the present, doubting of the rest?
    Love is a babe: then might I not say so,
    To give full growth to that which still doth grow.

一一五

我以前写给你的诗是瞎说，
说我无法爱你更深的那些诗都是谎。
当时我的理智不了解为了什么
我的热情以后会燃烧得更为明朗。
只是想到“时间”，他让无数次的变故
爬进盟誓之间，改变帝王们的命令，
污损神圣的美，消磨最猛利的雄图，
牵引最刚毅的人走上无常的路程。
哎呀！既然惧怕“时间”的暴力，
那么在我最有把握的时间
当时为何不说，“现在我最爱你”，
奉现在为至上，其他都不必管？
　　爱是婴儿。当时我不可这样说明，
　　把正在生长的东西看作完全长成[87]。

Sonnet 116

Let me not to the marriage of true minds
Admit impediments; love is not love
Which alters when it alteration finds,
Or bends with the remover to remove.
O no, it is an ever–fixèd mark
That looks on tempests and is never shaken;
It is the star to every wand'ring bark,
Whose worth's unknown, although his heighth be taken.
Love's not Time's fool, though rosy lips and cheeks
Within his bending sickle's compass come;
Love alters not with his brief hours and weeks,
But bears it out even to the edge of doom.
    If this be error and upon me proved,
    I never writ, nor no man ever loved.

一一六[88]

我不承认两颗真心相恋
会遭遇阻挠。爱不算是爱，
如果发现情形改变就跟着改变[89]，
或看到对方变心就打算走开[90]。
啊，不！爱是永远坚定的明灯，
面对着风暴而永不摇荡；
爱是指引漂流船只的明星[91]，
其高度可测，其奥秘不可衡量。
爱不是“时间”的玩物，虽然朱唇粉颊
逃不脱他弯弯镰刀的割芟；
爱不跟随流转的韶光而起变化，
爱抵抗“时间”到世界末日的尽端。
　　假如这话不对，而且引我为证，
　　我算是没写过诗，没人有过爱情。

Sonnet 117

Accuse me thus: that I have scanted all
Wherein I should your great deserts repay,
Forgot upon your dearest love to call,
Whereto all bonds do tie me day by day;
That I have frequent been with unknown minds,
And given to time your own dear–purchased right;
That I have hoisted sail to all the winds
Which should transport me farthest from your sight.
Book both my wilfulness and errors down,
And on just proof surmise accumulate;
Bring me within the level of your frown,
But shoot not at me in your wakened hate;
    Since my appeal says I did strive to prove
    The constancy and virtue of your love.

一一七

这样指控我吧：你的情爱厚深，
而我竟把一切报答完全怠忽；
友谊的羁绊对我日益加紧，
而我忘记乞求你的爱对我赐福；
我和不相干的人们亲密过从，
随便送掉你高价购得的权利；
我扯起帆来接受各方面的风，
送我到离你最远的地方去。
记下我的执拗和错误，
在确证之外再加上揣测；
皱起你的眉头对准我发怒，
可别一时恨起而把我杀射：
　　因为我抗辩说，我确是想要测验
　　你的情爱是否坚贞不变。

Sonnet 118

Like as to make our appetites more keen
With eager compounds we our palate urge,
As to prevent our maladies unseen
We sicken to shun sickness when we purge:
Even so, being full of your ne'er–cloying sweetness,
To bitter sauces did I frame my feeding,
And, sick of welfare, found a kind of meetness
To be diseased ere that there was true needing.
Thus policy in love, t'anticipate
The ills that were not, grew to faults assured,
And brought to medicine a healthful state
Which, rank of goodness, would by ill be cured.
  But thence I learn, and find the lesson true,
  Drugs poison him that so fell sick of you.

一一八

像是为要使我们的胃口大开，
我们把辛辣的作料送上舌端；
又像预防潜伏的疾病到来，
我们服泻药，泻得委顿不堪；
同样地，饱饫了你永不变腻的温柔，
我就把苦汁当作了我的食粮；
过度地幸福了，在不需要的时候，
我觉得也正不妨小病一场。
于是，情场上的手段，原想预防
未发生的毛病，惹出了真的病症，
把健康之躯变成了医疗的对象，
由于健康太多，求疾病来治病。
　　但是从此我学到一项真的教训，
　　药能毒杀一个这样饱饫你的人。

Sonnet 119

What potions have I drunk of Siren tears
Distilled from limbecks foul as hell within,
Applying fears to hopes, and hopes to fears,
Still losing when I saw myself to win!
What wretched errors hath my heart committed,
Whilst it hath thought itself so blessèd never!
How have mine eyes out of their spheres been fitted
In the distraction of this madding fever!
O benefit of ill! now I find true
That better is by evil still made better,
And ruined love when it is built anew
Grows fairer than at first, more strong, far greater.
　So I return rebuked to my content,
　And gain by ills thrice more than I have spent.

一一九

我喝了什么女妖眼泪制的毒浆，
那蒸馏器皿有如地狱一般乌黑，
于是给希望以恐惧，给恐惧以希望，
自以为得到好处，实则长久吃亏！
在自以为得未曾有的快乐时期，
我的心犯了什么样的错误！
在情欲狂烧头昏脑乱之际，
我的眼睛如何地从眼眶中跳出[92]！
啊，堕落的益处！现在我明白了，
经过堕落，高尚的爱就更高尚，
破碎的爱等到重新造好，
比原来更美、更强、更辉煌。
　　我便是受过谴责死心塌地地回来，
　　由于堕落我获益比损失多了三倍。

Sonnet 120

That you were once unkind befriends me now,
And for that sorrow which I then did feel
Needs must I under my transgression bow,
Unless my nerves were brass or hammerèd steel.
For if you were by my unkindness shaken
As I by yours, y'have passed a hell of time,
And I, a tyrant, have no leisure taken
To weigh how once I suffered in your crime.
O that our night of woe might have rememb'red
My deepest sense, how hard true sorrow hits,
And soon to you, as you to me then, tend'red
The humble salve, which wounded bosoms fits!
    But that your trespass now becomes a fee;
    Mine ransoms yours, and yours must ransom me.

一二〇[93]

你当初对我薄情，现在于我有益，
否则我想起当时感到的痛苦，
必定会在悔过心情之下垮了下去，
除非我的筋肉有如钢筋铜骨。
你如果因我负心而感到震撼，
一如我受你的打击，你是吃了苦头。
我是粗人，没有用闲暇时间
去思量你当初变心我是怎样的感受。
但愿我的苦痛经验能使我不忘
深刻的悲哀给我怎样沉重的打击。
赶快像你曾经对待我一样，
把膏药敷到你受伤的心灵上去！
　　但是你的罪过如今成了赎罪费，
　　我的罪过赎了你的，你的该把我赎回来。

Sonnet 121

'Tis better to be vile than vile esteemed,
When not to be receives reproach of being,
And the just pleasure lost, which is so deemed
Not by our feeling but by others' seeing.
For why should others' false adulterate eyes
Give salutation to my sportive blood?
Or on my frailties why are frailer spies,
Which in their wills count bad what I think good?
No, I am that I am, and they that level
At my abuses reckon up their own;
I may be straight though they themselves be bevel;
By their rank thoughts my deeds must not be shown,
  Unless this general evil they maintain:
  All men are bad and in their badness reign.

一二一

宁可做错事，也胜似徒负恶名，
如果没有作恶而受人谴责，
正当的快乐不曾享受成，
自问无他，而别人认为做错[94]。
别人的虚伪淫秽的双眼
怎可以对我的情欲暗送秋波？
比我脆弱的人怎可窥探我的弱点，
把我以为好的偏认为是罪过？
不，我就是我，对我漫骂的人们
正是暴露他们自己的缺德：
他们自己不正，我可能是正直的人；
他们不该以小人之心对我揣测；
　　除非他们主张所有的人都是恶，
　　根据他们的恶德批判别人的过错。

Sonnet 122

Thy gift, thy tables, are within my brain
Full charactered with lasting memory,
Which shall above that idle rank remain
Beyond all date, even to eternity;
Or, at the least, so long as brain and heart
Have faculty by nature to subsist,
Till each to razed oblivion yield his part
Of thee, thy record never can be missed.
That poor retention could not so much hold,
Nor need I tallies thy dear love to score;
Therefore to give them from me was I bold,
To trust those tables that receive thee more:
    To keep an adjunct to remember thee
    Were to import forgetfulness in me.

一二二

你送给我的笔记本，在我心里
已经写得满满的，永不忘怀，
绝不是一些无聊的诗句，
将超越时间到达永恒的境界；
至少可以长期存在，只消
头脑和心胸保有生存的能力；
只消二者都没有把你忘掉，
有关你的记录就永不会被遗弃。
那薄薄的本子写不了多少，
我对你的爱亦无须一一列举；
所以我大胆地把它丢弃了，
我心中的本子能记载更多的你：
　　若靠备忘录才能忆起你来，
　　那便是默认我会把你忘怀。

Sonnet 123

No! Time, thou shalt not boast that I do change:
Thy pyramids built up with newer might
To me are nothing novel, nothing strange;
They are but dressings of a former sight.
Our dates are brief, and therefore we admire
What thou dost foist upon us that is old,
And rather make them born to our desire
Than think that we before have heard them told.
Thy registers and thee I both defy,
Not wond'ring at the present, nor the past,
For thy recòrds, and what we see, doth lie,
Made more or less by thy continual haste.
    This I do vow and this shall ever be:
    I will be true despite thy scythe and thee.

一二三

不，时间，你休夸说我也变了心。
你用新的技巧造起的建筑物[95]
在我看来并不奇异，不新鲜，
不过是以前老东西加了新的装束。
人生苦短，所以我们赞叹
你用混骗手段塞给我们的旧货，
宁可认为那适合我们的心愿，
不愿想以前早就听说过。
我看不起你的史纪和你自己，
不惊羡现在，也不惊羡以往。
因为你的记录和眼前一切都是假的，
是你匆忙之中编造的谎。
　　我发誓这样说，永远会是这样的；
　　我忠贞不渝，不怕你的镰刀和你。

Sonnet 124

If my dear love were but the child of state,
It might for Fortune's bastard be unfathered,
As subject to Time's love, or to Time's hate,
Weeds among weeds, or flowers with flowers gathered.
No, it was builded far from accident;
It suffers not in smiling pomp, nor falls
Under the blow of thrallèd discontent,
Whereto th'inviting time our fashion calls;
It fears not Policy, that heretic,
Which works on leases of short–numb'red hours,
But all alone stands hugely politic,
That it nor grows with heat, nor drowns with show'rs.
　To this I witness call the fools of Time,
　Which die for goodness, who have lived for crime.

一二四 [96]

如果我的热情只是势利的产物，
那就成了命运的私生子，没有爸爸，
任由世人喜爱，或任由世人憎恶，
与草同除的莠草，或与花同采的香花。
不，它决不是偶然地建立起来。
快乐得意的时候它不会冷淡，
失意闷损的打击之下也不垮台。
失意正是我们这种人之所难免，
它不怕阴谋，那诡计多端的东西
只能对短暂的事物发生作用；
它是明察一切，巍然独立，
不因温暖而生长，亦不因霪雨而致命。
　　我要趋炎附势的小人为我做证，
　　他们一生为恶，临终皈依善行[97]。

Sonnet 125

Were't aught to me I bore the canopy,
With my extern the outward honouring,
Or laid great bases for eternity,
Which proves more short than waste or ruining?
Have I not seen dwellers on form and favour
Lose all, and more, by paying too much rent,
For compound sweet forgoing simple savour,
Pitiful thrivers, in their gazing spent?
No, let me be obsequious in thy heart,
And take thou my oblation, poor but free,
Which is not mixed with seconds, knows no art
But mutual render, only me for thee.
  Hence, thou suborned informer! A true soul
  When most impeached stands least in thy control.

一二五[98]

那对我有何益处，我若把华盖擎举[99]，
毕恭毕敬地对人公开捧场，
或是企图因此而沽名钓誉？
其实虚名易灭比财产更易花光。
难道我没见过过分注重外表的人
因付租金太多而大大地亏空，
为繁重的装潢而舍平淡的精神，
成了为贪图观赏而破产的富翁？
不，让我在你心里匍匐膜拜吧，
接受我的献礼，菲薄但是诚恳，
其中没有羼杂，没有一点虚假，
只是互相推爱，我们心心相印。
　　所以，你这胡言乱道的攻讦者！
　　真诚的人最不怕你的诬告谰说。

Sonnet 126

O thou my lovely boy, who in thy power
Dost hold Time's fickle glass, his sickle, hour;
Who hast by waning grown, and therein show'st
Thy lovers withering, as thy sweet self grow'st;
If Nature (sovereign mistress over wrack),
As thou goest onwards still will pluck thee back,
She keeps thee to this purpose, that her skill
May Time disgrace, and wretched minutes kill.
Yet fear her, O thou minion of her pleasure,
She may detain, but not still keep, her treasure!
  Her audit (though delayed) answered must be,
  And her quietus is to render thee.

一二六 [100]

我的可爱的孩子，你能把握
“时间”的沙漏及其镰刀一挥的时刻；
你随时间的消耗而逐渐长成，
你的朋友们则日趋于凋零。
如果“自然”那一切毁灭的主宰，
看着你前进，总是把你拉回来，
她抓住你，不外是这样的用意，
她要手段使“时间”丢丑，使分秒死去。
你还是别信任她，你这受宠的人！
她也许把你暂留，但不会永久保存。
　　她纵然拖延，她的账终归要结的，
　　她的债务了结便是把你放弃。

Sonnet 127

In the old age black was not counted fair,
Or if it were it bore not beauty's name;
But now is black beauty's successive heir,
And beauty slandered with a bastard shame:
For since each hand hath put on Nature's power,
Fairing the foul with art's false borrowed face,
Sweet beauty hath no name, no holy bower,
But is profaned, if not lives in disgrace.
Therefore my mistress' brows are raven black,
Her eyes so suited, and they mourners seem
At such who not born fair no beauty lack,
Sland'ring creation with a false esteem:
  Yet so they mourn, becoming of their woe,
  That every tongue says beauty should look so.

一二七 [101]

从前黑肤色不算是标致，
即使算标致，也没有美的名声。
但如今黑获得美的合法继承的位置，
美反倒蒙上一层私生子的恶名。
因为每个人都施展自然的权力，
用一张假造的脸来美化丑。
美貌不被尊重，不复是神圣的，
是受了渎亵，如果不是蒙垢含羞。
所以我的爱人脸色黑似乌鸦[102]，
眼睛也是黑的，好像是在悼伤
那些人生来不美而美貌并不缺乏，
妄自逞能，侮辱自然创造的力量。
　　可是那悼伤的样子可真漂亮，
　　人人都说美就应该是这个模样。

Sonnet 128

How oft, when thou, my music, music play'st
Upon that blessèd wood whose motion sounds
With thy sweet fingers when thou gently sway'st
The wiry concord that mine ear confounds,
Do I envỳ those jacks that nimble leap
To kiss the tender inward of thy hand,
Whilst my poor lips, which should that harvest reap,
At the wood's boldness by thee blushing stand!
To be so tickled they would change their state
And situation with those dancing chips
O'er whom thy fingers walk with gentle gait,
Making dead wood more blest than living lips.
Since saucy jacks so happy are in this,
Give them thy fingers, me thy lips to kiss.

一二八

你是我的音乐，你每次按动
那有福的木键，随着你的玉指纤纤，
便发出音响，你每次轻轻操纵
弦乐和鸣使得我耳神迷乱，
我多么羡慕那些木键欢蹦乱跳[103]
吻着你的柔嫩的手掌，
而我可怜的嘴唇，应享那番收获，
却只能羞赧地看着木键对你猖狂！
我的唇也愿享受那种感触，
愿和那些木键交换地位与境遇，
因为你的玉指在他们身上轻轻抚摸，
使死木头比活嘴唇更有福气。
　　猖狂的木键既然享有这样的福分，
　　把你的手指给他们，把你的唇给我吻。

Sonnet 129

Th'expense of spirit in a waste of shame
Is lust in action, and till action, lust
Is perjured, murd'rous, bloody, full of blame,
Savage, extreme, rude, cruel, not to trust,
Enjoyed no sooner but despisèd straight,
Past reason hunted, and no sooner had,
Past reason hated as a swallowed bait
On purpose laid to make the taker mad:
Mad in pursuit, and in possession so,
Had, having, and in quest to have, extreme,
A bliss in proof, and proved, a very woe,
Before, a joy proposed, behind, a dream.
    All this the world well knows, yet none knows well
    To shun the heaven that leads men to this hell.

一二九[104]

肉欲的满足乃是精力之可耻的浪费。
在未满足之前，肉欲是狡诈而有祸害，
血腥的，而且充满了罪，
粗野无礼，穷凶极恶，不可信赖；
刚刚一满足，立即觉得可鄙；
猎取时如醉如狂，一旦得到，
竟又悔又恨，像是有人故意
布下了钓饵被你吞掉。
追求时有如疯狂，得到时也一样。
已得，正在得，尚未得，都太极端。
享受时恍若天堂，事过后是懊丧。
事前，悬想中的快乐；事后，梦一般。

　　这一切无人不知，但无人懂得彻底，
　　对这引人下地狱的天堂加以规避。

Sonnet 130

My mistress' eyes are nothing like the sun;
Coral is far more red than her lips' red;
If snow be white, why then her breasts are dun;
If hairs be wires, black wires grow on her head.
I have seen roses damasked, red and white,
But no such roses see I in her cheeks,
And in some perfumes is there more delight
Than in the breath that from my mistress reeks.
I love to hear her speak, yet well I know
That music hath a far more pleasing sound;
I grant I never saw a goddess go –
My mistress when she walks treads on the ground.
    And yet, by heaven, I think my love as rare
    As any she belied with false compare.

一三〇[105]

我情人的眼睛和太阳不能比；
珊瑚远比她的嘴唇红得多；
如果雪是白的，她的奶就是黑的；
如果发是金丝，她头上是一片乌黑。
我见过粉红色玫瑰，又白又红，
但在她腮上我看不见这样的玫瑰；
有些香水的香气之浓
胜过我情人口里吐出的气味；
我爱听她说话，但是我心里有数，
音乐有远为悦耳的声响；
我承认没见过天仙走路，
我的情人走路是踏在地上。
　　但是，天哪，我的爱人之美丽
　　正不下于被人妄相比拟的任何妇女。

Sonnet 131

Thou art as tyrannous, so as thou art,
As those whose beauties proudly make them cruel;
For well thou know'st to my dear doting heart
Thou art the fairest and most precious jewel.
Yet in good faith some say that thee behold,
Thy face hath not the power to make love groan;
To say they err, I dare not be so bold,
Although I swear it to myself alone.
And to be sure that is not false I swear,
A thousand groans but thinking on thy face
One on another's neck do witness bear
Thy black is fairest in my judgement's place.
    In nothing art thou black save in thy deeds,
    And thence this slander as I think proceeds.

一三一

像你这个样子，居然飞扬跋扈，
有如自恃貌美的人们一般残暴，
因为你知道对于我的痴心爱慕
你是最美的最珍贵的珠宝。
但有些见过你的人却老实地说
你的脸没有使爱人呻吟的力量。
我不敢公然地说他们错，
虽然我私下骂他们没有眼光。
为了证实我的咒骂没有错误，
一想到你的脸，千百次唉声叹气，
一个跟着一个地执行证人任务，
证明在我心目里黑是最美的。
　　除了你的行为，你没有黑的地方，
　　我想是从那里生出这样的诽谤。

Sonnet 132

Thine eyes I love, and they, as pitying me,
Knowing thy heart torment me with disdain,
Have put on black, and loving mourners be,
Looking with pretty ruth upon my pain.
And truly not the morning sun of heaven
Better becomes the grey cheeks of the east,
Nor that full star that ushers in the even
Doth half that glory to the sober west
As those two mourning eyes become thy face.
O let it then as well beseem thy heart
To mourn for me, since mourning doth thee grace,
And suit thy pity like in every part.
    Then will I swear beauty herself is black,
    And all they foul that thy complexion lack.

一三二

你的两只眼睛我爱，像是怜悯我，
知道你心中的鄙夷使我苦痛，
所以披上黑色，成为亲近的吊者，
对我的苦痛寄予无限的同情。
老实说，早晨太阳出现在天空，
不能更美化东方灰色的面庞，
为夜晚做先导的那一颗明星
也不能带给朴素的西方更多光芒，
若是比起你脸上配着的那双黑眼。
啊，那么在你心里也要一样
伤悼我吧，因为伤悼使你更好看，
给你各部分哀怜都穿同样的服装。
　　美本身是黑色的，我可这样赌咒，
　　没有你的肤色的人都是丑陋。

Sonnet 133

Beshrew that heart that makes my heart to groan
For that deep wound it gives my friend and me!
Is't not enough to torture me alone,
But slave to slavery my sweet'st friend must be?
Me from myself thy cruel eye hath taken,
And my next self thou harder hast engrossed:
Of him, myself, and thee I am forsaken,
A torment thrice threefold thus to be crossed.
Prison my heart in thy steel bosom's ward,
But then my friend's heart let my poor heart bail;
Whoe'er keeps me, let my heart be his guard,
Thou canst not then use rigour in my jail.
    And yet thou wilt, for I, being pent in thee,
    Perforce am thine, and all that is in me.

一三三[106]

使我心伤的那颗心真该受诅咒，
它给我的朋友和我以那样的重伤！
让我一人受苦难道还嫌不够，
我的爱友也必须受奴下奴的灾殃？
你的残酷的眼睛已经把我夺去，
你更残酷地把我的朋友加以独占。
我被他，被我自己，被你，所遗弃，
这苦痛实在是三倍三倍地难堪。
把我的心关在你的心胸的钢栏里，
让我的可怜的心包起我朋友的心[107]。
不管谁囚禁我，让我的心做他的牢狱[108]，
你便无法在我的牢狱里面发狠。

　　你还是会发狠，因为我被你关起，
　　我属于你，我心中一切都是你的[109]。

Sonnet 134

So now I have confessed that he is thine,
And I myself am mortgaged to thy will,
Myself I'll forfeit, so that other mine
Thou wilt restore to be my comfort still:
But thou wilt not, nor he will not be free,
For thou art covetous, and he is kind;
He learned but surety–like to write for me
Under that bond that him as fast doth bind.
The statute of thy beauty thou wilt take,
Thou usurer, that put'st forth all to use,
And sue a friend came debtor for my sake,
So him I lose through my unkind abuse.
    Him have I lost, thou hast both him and me;
    He pays the whole, and yet am I not free.

一三四 [110]

好，如今我既承认他属于你，
我自己也抵押给你，由你使唤，
那么我愿奉献自己，以便换取
你释放那另一个我来长久和我做伴；
但是你不肯放，他也不愿脱身，
因为你忒贪，他也忒心善；
他本是在我效忠券上做保证人，
竟把他自己也牢牢牵涉在里面。
你将根据美貌的卖据而没收担保，
你这唯利是图的放高利贷者，
为我负债的朋友你也一齐控告；
于是由于她欺负我而使我失去他。
　　我已失去他，你把他和我一齐霸占：
　　他已付了全额，而我仍不能免。

Sonnet 135

Whoever hath her wish, thou hast thy Will,
And Will to boot, and Will in overplus;
More than enough am I that vex thee still,
To thy sweet will making addition thus.
Wilt thou, whose will is large and spacious,
Not once vouchsafe to hide my will in thine?
Shall will in others seem right gracious,
And in my will no fair acceptance shine?
The sea, all water, yet receives rain still,
And in abundance addeth to his store;
So thou being rich in Will add to thy Will
One will of mine to make thy large Will more.
    Let no unkind, no fair beseechers kill;
    Think all but one, and me in that one Will.

一三五 [111]

不管别人如何，你是欲望满足了，
加上一个威廉，再加上一个威廉。
我是太嫌过剩，总是引起你烦恼，
这样地撩拨你的欲火情焰。
你的欲壑真是宽大广深，
可否容我进去销魂一番？
你以为别人都是可爱可亲，
而你偏偏不肯和我缱绻？
大海全是水，仍然把雨承受下来，
大量地增加它的容量；
你的欲望大，在你的威廉之外
加上我的一份爱，扩大你的欲望。
　　不要用无情的“不”杀死忠实顾客。
　　对大家一视同仁，把我算作其中一个。

Sonnet 136

If thy soul check thee that I come so near,
Swear to thy blind soul that I was thy Will,
And will thy soul knows is admitted there;
Thus far for love, my love–suit, sweet, fulfil.
Will will fulfil the treasure of thy love,
Ay, fill it full with wills, and my will one.
In things of great receipt with ease we prove
Among a number one is reckoned none:
Then in the number let me pass untold,
Though in thy store's account I one must be;
For nothing hold me, so it please thee hold
That nothing me, a something sweet to thee.
    Make but my name thy love, and love that still,
    And then thou lovest me for my name is Will.

一三六

你的心灵若怪你容我这样热情，

告诉你那瞎眼的心灵我本是你的威廉，

你心里明白，你对情人是一律欢迎。

我热情追求如今总算是如了愿，

威廉会填满你的爱情的宝库，

是的，填得满满的，我也有一份。

我们有过经验，对于数字大的账目，

加上一个进去没有什么要紧；

虽然在你的总账里我要算一个，

且让我随着大家混了进去；

你可以不必怎样地重视我，

但你要承认我这区区是你的好东西[112]：

　　只消爱我的名字，并且爱得永远，

　　你就等于是爱我，因为我名叫威廉。

Sonnet 137

Thou blind fool, Love, what dost thou to mine eyes,
That they behold, and see not what they see?
They know what beauty is, see where it lies,
Yet what the best is take the worst to be.
If eyes, corrupt by over–partial looks,
Be anchored in the bay where all men ride,
Why of eyes' falsehood hast thou forgèd hooks,
Whereto the judgement of my heart is tied?
Why should my heart think that a several plot,
Which my heart knows the wide world's common place?
Or mine eyes seeing this, say this is not,
To put fair truth upon so foul a face?
In things right true my heart and eyes have erred,
And to this false plague are they now transferred.

一三七

你这瞎眼的爱神，你对我的双目
做了什么手脚，使得我瞪着眼看不见？
它们知道美是什么，美在何处居住，
但仍然把最丑恶的当作了最良善。
如果眼睛是偏爱美色受了骗诱，
于是在大众碇泊的湾港里抛锚，
你为什么以眼睛的虚幻做钓钩，
把我心中的理性也给系牢？
我的心明知那是大众共享的土地，
为什么还要认作是私人的地产？
为什么我亲眼看到而仍不措意，
以至于把美貌硬派给这样丑的脸？
　　我的心和眼错过了真正的美妇人，
　　如今活该对这个丑东西一见倾心。

Sonnet 138

When my love swears that she is made of truth,
I do believe her, though I know she lies,
That she might think me some untutored youth,
Unlearnèd in the world's false subtleties.
Thus vainly thinking that she thinks me young,
Although she knows my days are past the best,
Simply I credit her false–speaking tongue:
On both sides thus is simple truth suppressed.
But wherefore says she not she is unjust?
And wherefore say not I that I am old?
O love's best habit is in seeming trust,
And age in love loves not t'have years told.
    Therefore I lie with her, and she with me,
    And in our faults by lies we flattered be.

一三八 [113]

我的爱人发誓说她是一片忠贞，
我信任她，虽然我知道她说谎话，
好让我以为我是没经验的年轻人，
尚不懂人世间的虚伪和狡诈。
妄想她是以为我年轻易与，
虽然她知道我已过了盛年，
我却佯为信赖她的花言巧语，
于是双方都没有以诚相见。
为什么她不说她不忠贞？
为什么我不说我已衰老？
啊，爱的最佳外表便是貌似忠心，
老人在爱中不喜欢计算年纪大小。
　　所以我骗她，她也骗我，
　　用谎言彼此把缺点瞒过。

Sonnet 139

O call not me to justify the wrong
That thy unkindness lays upon my heart;
Wound me not with thine eye but with thy tongue;
Use power with power, and slay me not by art.
Tell me thou lov'st elsewhere; but in my sight,
Dear heart, forbear to glance thine eye aside;
What need'st thou wound with cunning when thy might
Is more than my o'erpressed defence can bide?
Let me excuse thee: 'Ah, my love well knows
Her pretty looks have been mine enemies,
And therefore from my face she turns my foes,
That they elsewhere might dart their injuries.'
　Yet do not so, but since I am near slain,
　Kill me outright with looks, and rid my pain.

一三九 [114]

啊，不要让我原谅你的冷漠
在我心上所留下来的委屈！
莫用你的眼睛伤我，用你的舌。
狠狠使用你的力量，杀我莫用狡计。
告诉我你另有所欢，但当我在你身旁，
亲爱的，不要对别人眉来眼去。
你何必用计害人，在你的力量
压迫之下我岂能有所抗拒？
我这样原谅你吧：“啊，我的爱人明白
她的美目流盼一直是我的敌人；
所以她把我的敌人从我脸上移开，
好教它们到别处去摄魄勾魂。”
　　但不可如此，我既已几乎丧命，
　　索性用目光杀我，免除我的苦痛。

Sonnet 140

Be wise as thou art cruel, do not press
My tongue–tied patience with too much disdain,
Lest sorrow lend me words, and words express
The manner of my pity–wanting pain.
If I might teach thee wit, better it were,
Though not to love, yet, love, to tell me so –
As testy sick men, when their deaths be near,
No news but health from their physicians know.
For if I should despair, I should grow mad,
And in my madness might speak ill of thee;
Now this ill–wresting world is grown so bad,
Mad slanderers by mad ears believèd be.
　That I may not be so, nor thou belied,
　Bear thine eyes straight, though thy proud heart go wide.

一四〇

你要像你残忍那样一般地明智；
我已张口结舌地忍耐，别逼人太甚；
否则悲哀要使我说话，会要表示
我是如何地因失宠爱而苦闷。
如果我可以教你机智，爱人，
你虽不爱我，最好还是说爱我的；
有如急躁的病人，死期已近，
从医生口里只能听到康复的消息；
因为如果我绝望，我会要发狂，
疯狂中会要说你的坏话：
如今世人专会往坏处想，
疯狂的耳朵相信疯狂的咒骂。
　　为了我不被人相信，你不受诽谤，
　　你的眼睛要对准我，虽然你的雄心远扬。

Sonnet 141

In faith, I do not love thee with mine eyes,
For they in thee a thousand errors note,
But 'tis my heart that loves what they despise,
Who in despite of view is pleased to dote.
Nor are mine ears with thy tongue's tune delighted,
Nor tender feeling to base touches prone,
Nor taste, nor smell, desire to be invited
To any sensual feast with thee alone;
But my five wits nor my five senses can
Dissuade one foolish heart from serving thee,
Who leaves unswayed the likeness of a man,
Thy proud heart's slave and vassal wretch to be.
    Only my plague thus far I count my gain,
    That she that makes me sin awards me pain.

一四一

老实说，靠眼睛我并不爱你，
因为在你身上我发现千种缺陷。
但是眼睛看不起的，我的心却有爱意。
虽然外表不扬，我心中却在热恋。
我的耳朵听了你的声音也不感愉快，
我也无意恣情抚摸你的肉体，
我的味觉嗅觉都不希望受你招待，
单独地和你共享肉欲的筵席，
但是我的五种心智五种官能[115]
不能打断我爱你的一片痴心。
于是我六神无主，徒具人形，
为你的雄心做奴隶，做卑贱的仆人。
　　我受苦难至今，只有一项好处，
　　她使我犯了罪，也给了我痛苦[116]。

Sonnet 142

Love is my sin, and thy dear virtue hate,
Hate of my sin, grounded on sinful loving.
O but with mine compare thou thine own state,
And thou shalt find it merits not reproving,
Or if it do, not from those lips of thine,
That have profaned their scarlet ornaments,
And sealed false bonds of love as oft as mine,
Robbed others' beds' revènues of their rents.
Be it lawful I love thee as thou lov'st those
Whom thine eyes woo as mine impòrtune thee:
Root pity in thy heart, that when it grows
Thy pity may deserve to pitied be.
    If thou dost seek to have what thou dost hide,
    By self–example mayst thou be denied.

一四二

爱是我的罪过，恨是你的德行，
你由于罪过的爱而恨我的罪过。
啊，只消把你的处境比比我的处境，
你就会觉得你原不该怪我；
如果该怪，也不该出诸你的嘴唇，
因为你已经渎亵了那朱红的外衣，
像我一样和别人已经频频接吻，
横夺了别的女人床笫上的收益。
我爱你和你爱别人一样地正当，
你向他们献媚犹如我之追求你。
你要培植悯怜心，一旦它发扬滋长，
你也会收到别人的怜悯的。
　　你自己若是靳而不与，反向别人乞讨，
　　依你自己的榜样你活该被人拒绝了！

Sonnet 143

Lo, as a careful huswife runs to catch
One of her feathered creatures broke away,
Sets down her babe and makes all swift dispatch
In pùrsuit of the thing she would have stay,
Whilst her neglected child holds her in chase,
Cries to catch her whose busy care is bent
To follow that which flies before her face,
Not prizing her poor infant's discontent:
So runn'st thou after that which flies from thee,
Whilst I, thy babe, chase thee afar behind;
But if thou catch thy hope, turn back to me,
And play the mother's part, kiss me, be kind.
  So will I pray that thou mayst have thy Will,
  If thou turn back and my loud crying still.

一四三

看，像是一位劳苦的妇人跑着追赶

她的逃走了的一只小鸡，

她放下了她的婴孩不管，

急急忙忙追逐她所要抓到的东西；

被抛下的婴孩又把她来追，

大哭大喊地想抓住她不放；

她一心追鸡，鸡在她前面飞，

可怜的婴孩啼叫，她不放在心上。

你便是这样追逐舍你而去的人，

我是在你后面追赶的那个孩提。

如果你能如愿以偿，请转回身

做个好母亲，吻我，亲亲热热地。

　　我愿祈祷你能获得你的“威廉”，

　　如果你肯回来止住我的啼喊。

Sonnet 144

Two loves I have, of comfort and despair,
Which like two spirits do suggest me still:
The better angel is a man right fair;
The worser spirit a woman coloured ill.
To win me soon to hell my female evil
Tempteth my better angel from my side,
And would corrupt my saint to be a devil,
Wooing his purity with her foul pride.
And whether that my angel be turned fiend
Suspect I may, yet not directly tell,
But being both from me, both to each friend,
I guess one angel in another's hell.
    Yet this shall I ne'er know, but live in doubt,
    Till my bad angel fire my good one out.

一四四[117]

我有两个爱人，给我慈悲与灾难[118]，
像是永久缠着我的两个呵护神：
善的精灵是个白净的男子汉，
恶的精灵是个黑脸儿的妇人。
我的女恶鬼为使我快快作恶，
诱使我的善天使不近我的身，
蛊惑我的圣徒变成了恶魔，
用她的丑模样迷惑他的天真。
我的天使是否变成了魔鬼了，
我疑心，可还不敢确定地说；
二者都不在我的身边，而且很要好，
我猜一个必已钻进另一个的窝[119]。
　　但此事我无法确知，我只能阙疑，
　　等着我的恶精灵传给他一身恶疾[120]。

Sonnet 145

Those lips that Love's own hand did make
Breathed forth the sound that said 'I hate'
To me that languished for her sake;
But when she saw my woeful state,
Straight in her heart did mercy come,
Chiding that tongue that ever sweet
Was used in giving gentle doom,
And taught it thus anew to greet:
'I hate' she altered with an end
That followed it as gentle day
Doth follow night, who like a fiend
From heaven to hell is flown away:
'I hate' from hate away she threw,
And saved my life, saying 'not you'.

一四五 [121]

爱神亲手造的那两片唇，
对着为伊人而憔悴的我
吐出了声音说：“我恨。”
但是听到我为失恋而难过，
慈悲立刻涌上她的心端，
骂那惯于发布温柔消息，
一向甜蜜蜜的舌尖，
教它把话重新这样说起：
她给“我恨”加了一个句尾，
于是有如白昼接上了夜晚，
夜晚像是一个魔鬼，
从天堂往地狱里逃窜。
　　她把一声“我恨”撇得全无恶意，
　　她救了我一命，说：“恨的不是你。”

Sonnet 146

Poor soul, the centre of my sinful earth,
[. . .] these rebel powers that thee array,
Why dost thou pine within and suffer dearth
Painting thy outward walls so costly gay?
Why so large cost, having so short a lease,
Dost thou upon thy fading mansion spend?
Shall worms, inheritors of this excess,
Eat up thy charge? Is this thy body's end?
Then, soul, live thou upon thy servant's loss,
And let that pine to aggravate thy store;
Buy terms divine in selling hours of dross;
Within be fed, without be rich no more:
    So shalt thou feed on Death, that feeds on men,
    And Death once dead, there's no more dying then.

一四六

可怜的灵魂，我的顽躯的中心，
被包围你的叛变的血肉所玩耍[122]，
你为什么内心憔悴，忍受饥馑，
你的外墙却粉饰得那样豪华？
何必如此浪费？租期如此短暂，
对你行将腐朽的房屋还要开销？
是要蛆虫承继这一份豪华遗产
来把它吃掉？这是你肉体的目标？
灵魂哪，你要折磨你的躯体，
让它憔悴，以增加你的财富；
卖掉尘世光阴把永恒来换取；
心外无须富丽，内心需要滋补：
　　这样你便可吃掉那吃人的死神，
　　死神一死，再没有死令你担心。

Sonnet 147

My love is as a fever, longing still
For that which longer nurseth the disease,
Feeding on that which doth preserve the ill,
Th'uncertain sickly appetite to please.
My reason, the physician to my love,
Angry that his prescriptions are not kept,
Hath left me, and I desperate now approve
Desire is death, which physic did except.
Past cure I am, now reason is past care,
And, frantic mad with evermore unrest,
My thoughts and my discourse as madmen's are,
At random from the truth vainly expressed:
For I have sworn thee fair, and thought thee bright,
Who art as black as hell, as dark as night.

一四七

我的爱情像热病，总是渴望
能把病情维持得更长久，
把能保持疾病的东西当食粮，
以满足不正常不健康的胃口。
我的理智，我的爱情的医生，
为了我没有遵服他的处方，
一怒而去，我于绝望之中
领悟医家禁忌的肉欲即是死亡。
理智既已不管，我便无可救药，
只得愈益不安地发着狂癫；
我像疯人一般地胡想乱道，
任意地瞎扯，虚妄地歪缠：
　　我发誓说过你美，以为你皎洁，
　　其实你黑似地狱，暗似昏夜。

Sonnet 148

O me! what eyes hath love put in my head,
Which have no correspondence with true sight?
Or, if they have, where is my judgement fled,
That censures falsely what they see aright?
If that be fair whereon my false eyes dote,
What means the world to say it is not so?
If it be not, then love doth well denote
Love's eye is not so true as all men's: no,
How can it? O, how can love's eye be true,
That is so vexed with watching and with tears?
No marvel then though I mistake my view:
The sun itself sees not till heaven clears.
　O cunning love, with tears thou keep'st me blind,
　Lest eyes, well seeing, thy foul faults should find.

一四八

哎呀！爱神给了我什么样的眼睛，
竟没有与实物相符合的目光？
纵然有，何以判断力逃得无影无踪，
看得真切而批评不得其当？
我的昏花眼所迷恋的如果真是好，
何以世人都说那不见得妙？
如果不好，那么这段爱情表示了
情人眼睛不若大家的可靠：不可靠。
怎能可靠？彻夜失眠，泪水汪汪，
啊！情人眼睛怎能是可靠的？
难怪我看东西要看走了样。
除非晴空万里，太阳也看不见东西。
　　狡猾的爱人！你用泪水使我瞎了眼，
　　否则明察的眼睛会发现你的缺点。

Sonnet 149

Canst thou, O cruel, say I love thee not,
When I against myself with thee partake?
Do I not think on thee when I forgot
Am of myself, all tyrant for thy sake?
Who hateth thee that I do call my friend?
On whom frown'st thou that I do fawn upon?
Nay, if thou lour'st on me, do I not spend
Revenge upon myself with present moan?
What merit do I in myself respect
That is so proud thy service to despise,
When all my best doth worship thy defect,
Commanded by the motion of thine eyes?
    But, love, hate on, for now I know thy mind:
    Those that can see thou lov'st, and I am blind.

一四九

狠心的，你能说我对你不爱，
我已站在你一边反对我自身？
我没想你吗？为了你我已忘怀
我自己，你这蛮不讲理的人。
哪一个恨你的人我称之为友？
你对谁恼怒而我偏对他谄媚？
不，在你对我皱眉的时候，
我不立即愤然和我自己作对？
我发现了自己具备什么优点，
以致得意忘形不屑向你效忠，
实际上我在全力崇拜你的缺陷，
被你那秋波一转所操纵？
　　但是，爱人，你恨吧。我现在懂你的心理，
　　你爱的是那些有眼睛的，而我是瞎了眼的。

Sonnet 150

O from what pow'r hast thou this pow'rful might
With insufficiency my heart to sway,
To make me give the lie to my true sight,
And swear that brightness doth not grace the day?
Whence hast thou this becoming of things ill,
That in the very refuse of thy deeds
There is such strength and warrantise of skill
That in my mind thy worst all best exceeds?
Who taught thee how to make me love thee more,
The more I hear and see just cause of hate?
O, though I love what others do abhor,
With others thou shouldst not abhor my state.
    If thy unworthiness raised love in me,
    More worthy I to be beloved of thee.

一五〇

啊，你从什么神祇获得这股力量，
靠了缺陷而控制了我的心情？
使我不信我的真实可靠的眼光，
硬说白昼之美不在于光明？
你化丑陋为妩媚的力量哪里来的？
你的最无聊的行为里面
都有特殊的诱惑与魅力，
在我心中你的极恶超过一切至善。
谁教导你使我在听到看到
都该怀恨的时候愈发爱你？
啊，我爱的是别人所不敢领教，
你和别人都不必为我的迷惘而恐惧。
　　如果你的缺陷引起了我的爱，
　　我就更该受你的柔情款待。

Sonnet 151

Love is too young to know what conscience is,
Yet who knows not conscience is born of love?
Then, gentle cheater, urge not my amiss,
Lest guilty of my faults thy sweet self prove.
For thou betraying me, I do betray
My nobler part to my gross body's treason:
My soul doth tell my body that he may
Triumph in love; flesh stays no farther reason,
But rising at thy name doth point out thee
As his triumphant prize. Proud of this pride,
He is contented thy poor drudge to be,
To stand in thy affairs, fall by thy side.
    No want of conscience hold it that I call
    Her 'love' for whose dear love I rise and fall.

一五一

爱神太幼稚，本不解人事，
可是谁不知道爱情会导致奸情[123]？
那么，好骗子，别追究我的过失，
否则会证明你犯与我同样的罪行。
因为你骗了我，我也把
我较高贵部分卖给叛变的肉体；
我的灵魂对我的肉体发话，
他可以真个销魂；那块肉不再犹豫，
一听到你的名字就振作起来，指着你
做他的战利品。虽然威风不小，
他终归做了你的可怜的奴隶，
为你效劳，最后在你的身旁瘫倒。
　　我喊她作“爱”，为她而兴起而衰落，
　　不要认为这是没有良心的过错。

Sonnet 152

In loving thee thou know'st I am forsworn,
But thou art twice forsworn to me love swearing:
In act thy bed–vow broke, and new faith torn
In vowing new hate after new love bearing.
But why of two oaths' breach do I accuse thee,
When I break twenty? I am perjured most,
For all my vows are oaths but to misuse thee,
And all my honest faith in thee is lost.
For I have sworn deep oaths of thy deep kindness,
Oaths of thy love, thy truth, thy constancy,
And to enlighten thee gave eyes to blindness,
Or made them swear against the thing they see:
  For I have sworn thee fair: more perjured eye,
  To swear against the truth so foul a lie.

一五二

你知道我爱你乃是违反我的婚约，
但是自你发誓爱我，你背誓两度；
你先破坏你的婚约，又把新盟撕却，
对你的新欢又表示新的厌恶。
我背誓无数次，又何必斥责你
背誓两度？我食言的次数很勤，
因为我的誓言只是把你乱捧一气[124]，
我对你早已失去一切真诚的心：
我曾重重发誓，说你深深多情，
说你相爱，说你真诚，说你不变；
为了给你增光，我情愿瞎了眼睛，
让眼睛发誓说所见与实况相反。
　　因为我曾发誓说你美。是我的谎大[125]，
　　竟说出这样不符真相的假话！

Sonnet 153

Cupid laid by his brand and fell asleep:
A maid of Dian's this advantage found,
And his love–kindling fire did quickly steep
In a cold valley–fountain of that ground;
Which borrowed from this holy fire of Love
A dateless lively heat, still to endure,
And grew a seething bath, which yet men prove
Against strange maladies a sovereign cure.
But at my mistress' eye Love's brand new fired,
The boy for trial needs would touch my breast;
I, sick withal, the help of bath desired,
And thither hied, a sad distempered guest;
  But found no cure: the bath for my help lies
  Where Cupid got new fire – my mistress' eyes.

一五三 [126]

邱比得放下火把睡着了，
戴安娜的一位侍女有机可乘，
匆匆把他点燃爱情的火把浸泡
在那地方的一个冷泉当中，
泉水从这圣洁的爱情之火
获得永无尽期的热，永久不冷，
于是变成沸滚的温泉一座，
以后大家认为能治疑难杂症。
但我爱人眼里燃起新的爱情火把，
那孩子一定要在我胸上试验一番；
我立即病倒，想借温泉治疗一下，
跑到那边，心情苦恼，狼狈不堪，
　　但是发现无效：能救治我的温泉
　　乃是邱比得点燃新火把的地方，我爱人的双眼。

Sonnet 154

The little Love–god lying once asleep
Laid by his side his heart–inflaming brand,
Whilst many nymphs that vowed chaste life to keep
Came tripping by; but in her maiden hand
The fairest votary took up that fire
Which many legions of true hearts had warmed,
And so the general of hot desire
Was sleeping by a virgin hand disarmed.
This brand she quenchèd in a cool well by,
Which from Love's fire took heat perpetual,
Growing a bath and healthful remedy
For men diseased; but I, my mistress' thrall,
   Came there for cure, and this by that I prove:
   Love's fire heats water, water cools not love.

一五四

小爱神有一次在打瞌睡，
把点燃爱情的火把放在身边，
这时誓守贞操的小仙一队
轻轻地走来，最美的一位小仙
把那曾经点燃过无数
心头爱情的火把拿在手上，
于是这位热情的霸主
在睡中被一位贞女解除了武装。
她把这火把往附近冷泉里浸泡，
泉水由爱火获得永久的热力，
变成了温泉，而且能够治疗
人们的疾病。但是我，我爱人的奴隶，
　　走到那里治疗，只得到这样的证明：
　　爱火可以烧热了水，水不能冷却爱情。

注释

[1] 此一著名献词原文如下:

TO. THE. ONLIE. BEGETTER. OF.

THESE. INSUING. SONNETS.

Mr. W. H. ALL. HAPPINESSE.

AND. THAT. ETERNITIE.

PROMISED.

BY.

OUR. EVER-LIVING. POET.

WISHETH.

THE. WELL-WISHING.

ADVENTURER. IN.

SETTING.

FORTH.

T.T.

这是用碑碣体裁写的，所以每一字后有一圆点，而且文字也很矜持。按照正常英文语法，应该是这样的："To the only begetter of these ensuing sonnets，Mr.W.H.，the well-wishing adventurer in setting forth wisheth all happiness and that eternity promised by our ever-living poet,（signed）T.T."。有人把 Mr. W.H. 当作句子的主词，那似乎是讲不通的。这一段献词颇有晦涩难明之处，例如何谓 only begetter，谁是 Mr. W.H.，何谓 adventurer in setting forth，谁是 T.T. 等等，请参阅序文。

[2] 第一首至第十七首，自成段落，是写给一位青年的，劝他结婚以便生男育女使他的美貌长留永久不朽。这种想法并不奇特，人到中年看到人生无常，自有无穷感喟，唯有子息的繁衍才是生命的延长。

[3] "四十个冬天"，言年届四十的时候，不是再过四十年之意。莎氏写此诗时年约三十。

[4] all-eating shame and thriftless praise，Pooler 释为"the shame of gluttony and the praise of extravagance，since you devour the world's due and are an unthrift of your beauty"，是也。Prof. Dowden 释 thriftless 为 unprofitable，恐不恰。

[5] 言不肯与女人来往。

[6] 按照伊利沙白女王所恢复的亨利八世时的法令，最高的合法利率是百分之十。此处所谓 ten for one 应该是百分之一千了。

[7]conquest 不是武力占领之意，是“经由继承以外方法而得来之产业，为heritage之对待语”（OED）。

[8]thyself outgoing in thy noon，Beeching 注："passing beyond thy meridian beauty，and so declining"，是也。outgoing 不宜作不及物动词解。

[9]“如照字面解释，此诗前四行提供了有关 W.H. 先生之有趣的资料:（一）不仅貌美，且有悦耳的声音；（二）他喜爱音乐，但似《威尼斯商人》中之杰西卡，‘听到美妙乐声即为之不欢’。”（威尔孙）“此诗所用之譬喻系指琵琶弹奏（luteplaying）。为充分了解起见，吾人必须记得琵琶之弦，除最高音是单弦外，均系两弦成对的同时弹奏。”（Campbell）

[10] 原版四开本 For shame 二字之后无任何标点，近代编本率于二字之后加逗点或感叹号，似无必要，for shame = for shame's sake 加强语气之意。

[11]departest 一般解作 leave behind，意指“青春”而言。Beeching 注: departest = separatest off，that which thou departest = a slip of thee，似较胜。前两行大意，Ingram & Redpath 释作“Out of that seed

which I am asking you to sow, you will grow, in a child of your making, as fast as you decline in yourself."。

[12] 原版 Look 后无 comma。Look whom 应解作 whomever。the more 想系 thee more 之误。全句大意是"To whomsoever Nature gave her best she gave thee more."。(威尔孙)

[13]that copy = the original seal。

[14] 指诗人所作之诗篇。

[15]to give away yourself 可能兼具"to give yourself in marriage"及"to produce likeness of yourself"二者之含义。

[16] 前十七首大意是劝朋友结婚生子以保持其容貌美德于不朽。自第八首至二十六首又成一段落，诗人率直表示了爱慕之情，以诗篇使他的朋友名垂于永久。

[17] 葛来高利历法施行以前之五月，实际延展到现在之六月中旬数日，属于夏季。

[18] 这是唯一使用"双音节脚韵"(double rhymes)的一首诗。词意粗率，似非一戏剧演员对一贵族青年所宜有之口吻，但当时风尚，不以为忤也。

[19] 莎士比亚写此诗时只有三十多岁，不能说老，但

"叹老"是十四行诗作者们的惯习。

[20] 哈姆雷特的剧中剧，在演员上台之前即先有哑剧一场预告剧中情节。故此处所谓 dumb presagers 应即是 preliminary dumb shows。

[21]Ingram & Redpath 提供的意见是对的，pèrspective 应作为副词解，即 perspectively，亦即"seen from the right angle" or "seen through the appropriate optical glass"之意，全句大意为"Shakespeare is not saying that such clever projections are the highest form of pictorial art，but that his heart's image of the Friend is a perfect portrait，though to realize this we must see it through the poet's eye."。

[22] 此诗语气似为"献词"性质，第三行所谓 written ambassage（强调非口头传述而是见诸文字），可能指第十八首至第二十五首这一束情诗。绝不是指第二十六首本诗而言，更不该因在文字上近似 Lucrece 一诗之献词而指为与 Lucrece 有关之献诗。

[23] 四开本原文 their respect，近代本自 Capell 以降多改为 thy respect。

[24] 第二十七至四十七首，成一段落。O. J. Campbell 做如下之撮要:"诗人似在出外旅行

（二十七至三十二首）。也许在他出游时，发现他的年轻贵人略诱了他的情人，或被他的情人所诱惑（三十三至四十七首）。莎士比亚责友不义，使之悔恨流泪（三十四首）。其友既悔过，诗人即宽恕之，对其仪容财富以及门第才华仍然倾倒备至。但至撰写第四十首诗时，其友又复与其情人发生性的关系。此乃'第二度犯过'。诗人再度宽恕之，反责情人之诱惑力太大。在第四十二首里诗人控制情感，居然能强词自解。他告诉情人，他与友人虽形体分离，心灵则融而为一，她爱那青年实即爱他自己也。”

[25]Pooler 注云:“此诗背后的事实是:（一）莎士比亚因与爱友暌违，忆起了其他已故的知交;（二）他的暌违的朋友荟萃了所有死友的优点;（三）莎士比亚对他的情谊乃是对于其他故交的情谊之总和。”第一行之 hearts 似宜解作“知心的友人”。

[26]“死亡”被拟为掘坟墓的乡下人。

[27]Tyler 注云:“我们可以揣想，现在另一系列的十四行诗开始了。莎士比亚不在的时候，W.H. 先生可能和诗人的异性朋友即第一百二十七诸首中之黑女郎，过度亲密。诗人归后 W.H. 先生有若干疏冷之表现。过去友谊有如夏晨之骄阳，如今则太阳为彤云所笼罩。诗人仍不因灰心而绝交。天仍有放晴之望也。”

[28] 四开本原文第八行是: Excusing their sins more than their sins are，句费解，近代本多改 their 为 thy，牛津本亦然。实则以不改为是，全首意义简单而一贯，无须多加臆测横生枝节。所谓 their，指第二、三、四各行之玫瑰、泉源等而言也，盖谓此等事物无心为恶，与友人之夺人之爱者不可相提并论，诗人引为比喻，实乃比拟不伦，陷于错误。其意若曰: “Excusing their sins as something more than they really are.”。Ingram & Redpath 的解释最为允洽: “All men commit errors，and，in fact，I am doing so in trying to justify your misconduct by drawing analogies（in the first quatrain），thus corrupting myself in palliating your offence，since I am by implification exonerating those natural objects from a moral turpitude they are incapable of（thus confusing the natrual and moral orders）.”。

[29] 这一首颇为费解。为什么诗人和他的朋友必须分散？第三行的 blots 与第十行的 bewailèd guilt 何所指？是否指同一件事？细玩语气，与第三十五首是不连贯的。而且在韵律上，第三十六至三十九首这四首诗自然形成为一集团，威尔孙特别明显地指出这四

首的韵脚连贯的情形:

36	1	twain	3	remain		37	1	delight	3	spite
	2	one	4	alone			10	give	12	live
	6	spite	8	delight			13	thee	14	me
	9	thee	11	me						
38	5	me	7	thee		39	2	me	4	thee
	6	sight	8	light			5	live	7	give
							6	one	8	alone
							13	twain	14	remain

这四首自成体系，可能是应该排印在另外一个位置，有人主张这四首应该紧跟着第二十九首，威尔孙认为应该更往前提，放在第二十五首之后。据传统的解释，所谓“耻辱”和“罪过”是指诗人身份与他的朋友身份悬殊，诗人为一普通演员，故叹贫嗟卑自怨自艾（参看第二十九首第一行）。威尔孙以为出身低微不能算是罪过，诗人坚欲与友分离应另有原因在，可能是因为一五九七年天鹅剧院上演一出被认为有煽动性的戏《狗岛》（*The Isle of Dogs*），触怒当道，剧院被封，涉及该剧者悉数被捕，而莎士比亚可能亦被株连在内。此说有其可能，惜无佐证。Campbell 注:“二人同爱一女显然已成众所周知之事。按照文艺复兴的交友之道，严格讲，诗人不可默默地与人争风，应拱手奉让，一如《维洛那二绅士》之瓦伦坦将西尔维亚让给普罗提阿斯……”此说为另一解释，以此诗为第三十五首之延续。译者之意，原诗措辞既含

糊不清，译时亦不必遵从任何一家之说而做明确之解说也。

[30] approve 有双关义：（一）尝试，可能暗指性方面的享受；（二）怀有好感，赏识。

[31] 第四十三至四十五首意义相连。诗人写至第四十三首，诗意似已穷竭，只好效法皮特拉克一派，乞灵于“奇想”conceit。shadow 一字有数义。

[32]darkly bright = secretly cheerful。are bright in dark directed = can see clearly what they are looking at in the dark。（Wilson）

[33] 六至八行，Ingram & Redpath 注：i.e. “How your body，brighter than the day，would add a fitting splendour to the day's brightness.”。

[34] 指莎氏时代一般人所信的 Galen 一派的生理学所谓四元素之说，土与水二元素是重滞的，气与火是轻灵的。思想是气，或气与火二者之混合物，故肉体是重滞的，思想是轻灵的。

[35] 诗人之眼与心涉讼公堂，心是原告，眼是被告，但所争何事？依第三行及下一首第五、第六行所云，显然有一幅画像牵涉在内，双方所争者似为享有此画像之权利。陪审员之判决，不特偏袒，且不对题。

[36] 四十八至六十六首为一单位，描写诗人别后之

忧虑。

[37] 指合伙人之拆伙。

[38] 原文 And this my hand against myself uprear，自 Beeching 至 Wilson 大都以为是在法庭举手宣誓做证之意。Ingram & Redpath 注云："此数行历来各家解释吾人以为完全错误，诗人不是为人攻击自己而到法庭做证，根本不是在做证。他是在根据自我认识而为自己辩护，抵抗他的朋友可能提出之冷淡他的理由。他承认他的朋友有权随时遗弃他，但此权利乃是根据一项消极事实，即他自己本无可爱之处，而不是根据任何该受谴责之积极理由。"此说似是。against 在此处应解作 in front of。

[39] But love，for love，费解。Ingram & Redpath 注："But love itself，out of its own inherent charity."，似较恰。

[40] 阿都尼斯（Adonis），希腊神话中之美少年。海伦（Helen），希腊神话中之美女。

[41] 马尔斯（Mars），战神。

[42] 九至十二行，费解。有人以为指 Hero 与 Leander 之隔海相恋的故事，有人以为海洋系泛喻任何使情人们隔离的障碍物，甚至有人提出那是死亡。无论怎样解释，所谓"Return of love"与海洋

难以连贯。

[43] 四开本作 in your Will，其中之 Will 系大写，有人以为 Will 即是 William Shakespeare 之意，但细玩语气恐未必然。有人以为 will=sexual desire，亦嫌穿凿。

[44] 每隔三万五千年或四万九千年，天道循环一次，一切事物重演，这是古代的一种信仰。亚里士多德的学生 Eudemus 说："如是我们相信 Pythagoreans 的学说，目前情况将来会将重演，我目前手持教鞭在课堂上课，若干年后，同样情形将丝毫不差地重复演出。"斯多亚派哲学家 Marcus Aurelius 说："太阳之下无新物。"莎士比亚在本诗引用此项见解，其目的在说明今人胜古人也。第六行所谓五百年亦即天文学上所谓 Great Year 或 Platonic Year 之另一说法。

[45] And for myself mine own worth do define 费解，困难在于句中无主词，在 do 字前的 I 是被省略了，可能是由于第五行之 Methinks 已含有"我"的意义在内。

[46] 参看《哈姆雷特》三幕一景之著名的"To be or not to be"一段独白。Dowden 注："莎士比亚由忧虑朋友之死转而想到自己之死，并想到人生苦恼重重，唯一死可得解脱。"上述一段独白及此诗常被认

为是莎士比亚本人内心之呼声。

[47] 六十七至七十四首为一段落，主题为“丑恶与死亡”。六十七首里提到脂粉化妆品，莎士比亚一向是反对脂粉和假发的，参看《哈姆雷特》三幕一景一四五行，《第十二夜》一幕五景二四〇行。但在此诗仅是顺笔提到此一时髦，表示他的朋友之无须乞灵于脂粉，并非指责他的朋友有此恶习也。全诗主旨在最后四行。

[48] 原文 dead seeing，四开本如此，近代本（包括牛津本在内）多从之，今照译。其意一般解释为 false appearance，义可通，惜无强有力之根据。Capell 改为 seeming，近代本如 Wilson 与 Ingram & Redpath 皆从之。

[49] 原文 itself and true，其中之 itself 费解。Ingram & Redpath 主张 itself 应分写为 it self，以 self 为形容词，颇有见地。唯 it 应是指 antique hours 而言。（如 Pooler 所指陈，表示时间之复数形名词应作为单数解。）

[50] 所谓作品（that which I bring forth），可能指此诗，可能指所有的诗作，亦可能是指为剧院所编写之戏剧。以贵族而与演戏人员密切交游在当时是不体面的。

[51] 原　文 The coward conquest of a wretch's knife，费解。wretch 是谁？一般解释为“死神”或“时间”。Dowden 揣测可能与 Marlowe 之在酒店被人杀死之事有关，威尔孙亦倾向此说。又谓可能指莎士比亚有欲寻短见之意。俱属臆测，了无凭证。

[52] 第七十五至九十九首为一段落，其主题为“友谊遭遇之危机”。

[53] 诗中所谓“时髦作风”，可能有所指。威尔孙谓可能指 Chapman，Campbell 谓可能指 John Donne 之早年作品。

[54]“斯蒂芬斯所谓此诗‘是为陪伴一件空白小册的礼物而制’，好像几乎是确切之论。像这样的一件礼物，在莎士比亚时代和在斯蒂芬斯时代，都是稀松平常不足为奇的，而且也是很有价值的，不若我们现代所感觉的那样奇怪，此种礼物在古董市场尚常出现。镜子与日晷是否亦为礼物之一部分，不能确定，不过所谓 thy glass 与 thy dial 似是暗示并非其中之一部分。”（Ingram & Redpath 注）

[55] 第四行末之标点原为句点，如 Ingram & Redpath 之所指陈，以改冒号为宜。

[56]“这些事物”指镜子与日晷，所谓“作用”指镜子与日晷在朋友心中所引起之感想，而这些感想将记

载在此一空白册内。

[57] 在此诗中莎士比亚明白提起一位和他竞争的诗人，究竟是谁则不能确定，或谓为班章孙，或谓Chapman，总之是一位比莎士比亚学殖较深地位较高之人，故称之为“学者”，而“冥顽”“哑巴”则是莎士比亚自谦之词。第七行所谓“把羽毛加在学者的翅上”，系引用鹰猎术语，鹰翅羽毛残缺时则加以移植补贴云。

[58]“两个诗人”（both your poets）可能指:（一）莎士比亚及另一争宠的诗人;（二）两个和莎士比亚争宠的诗人。第十二行之 others 系复数形，后一解或较合理。

[59] 前四行标点有问题，故释义亦有歧异。四开本在前四行内用了七个逗点（most，more，praise, alone, you, store, grew, ），正如 Pooler 之所指陈，这显然是“表示节奏而不是表示意义”，他进一步揣测“也许唯一的问号应该放在 grew 后面”，可是他并未这样改窜。今按牛津本译。

[60]Ingram & Redpath 注:“reserve 与 character 二字若按照伊利沙白时代的训义，则第三四两行可做如是之解释:‘Store up manuscript upon manuscript，writing them in letters of gold

and in choice phrases polished by learned study of the greatest poets.' Alternatively, line 3 could mean : 'lay up in permanent record their characteristic style (or styles) by writing in letters of gold choice phrases...'。"无论如何，reserve 一字无改动之必要; character 一字当作 "文字"解。

[61] 这些"伙伴"不知是谁，有人说是荷马及罗马诗人，也有人认为是 Marlowe、Chapman 等。第十行之"精灵"亦不知究何所指。

[62] 四开本的标点，第七行之 disgrace 与 will 后均为逗点，第八行之 strange 后为冒号。近代编本多加以变动，牛津本是在第七行之 disgrace 与第八行之 strange 均改为分号（semi-colon），在第七行之 will 后仍保留逗点。兹照 Ingram & Redpath 的意见，第七行 disgrace 后用逗点，will 后用冒号，第八行 strange 后用逗点。意义大有出入。

[63] 第五、第六两行意义晦涩。Campbell 注: "Then I need not fear the entire loss of your love when the first intimation of its loss would kill me."。Ingram & Redpath 注: "The least sign of coldness or inconstancy on your part will kill

me，so I need not fear to live to endure the worst wrong of all，complete alienation."。二说大致相同，较其他各家解释为佳。

[64] 最后两行与第三十六首最后两行重复。是莎士比亚有意如此，还是原稿缺残，编者如此借补，不可知。

[65] 第五、第六两行"summer's time"，"The teeming autumn"费解，引起不少评论。所谓 the teeming autumn 即是 summer's time，诗人与朋友别离在夏天，别离之后，不胜相思之苦，只得在回忆中度日，这夏天有如充满春日美丽回忆的秋天也。Ingram & Redpath 改第五行末之 semicolon 为 comma，dash 颇有见地。第九行 yet 语气一转，盖谓回忆固然可以自娱，然亦只是慰情聊胜于无，独自享受耳，如寡妇之抚爱其遗腹子也。

[66] 土星（Saturn），按星相学家说，是一个寒冷迟缓的行星，能增加忧郁症的黑胆汁。

[67] 这一首共十五行，在全集中是唯一例外，但在伊利沙白时代其他十四行诗集中此种情形亦屡有发现。这一首中任何一行皆不可删去而不伤及诗意，以韵脚而论第一行或第五行是多余的。

[68]"两者"可能是指红白二种颜色。

[69] 自第一百首至第一〇八首为一段落，诗人与友人之间的长期反目告一终止，诗人精神重振，又复肆力颂扬其友人之美。

[70] 真与美乃两个抽象的永恒的理想，人是无常的生物，我们通常说人靠理想而生存，这一行诗一反其道，谓理想乃是依靠人而存在，极言其人之如何高明也。

[71] Philomel，夜莺之别名，其歌声如哀诉，按神话及诗中引用均属雌性，实则能歌者为雄鸟。

[72] 威尔孙注云:“我的结论是，此诗乃为 Herbert 二十岁生日（一六〇〇年四月八日）作，诗中所谓之‘三年’正好说明二人初遇是在一五九七年四月八日，亦即 Herbert 的十七岁生日。”

[73]Three April perfumes in three hot Junes burned，此句读来拗口，但甚有力。意为三次春天变成了三次盛夏，至为明显，但 perfumes、burned 喻义安在？ Beeching 以为是以投香入火为喻，Tucker 更进一步以为是投香入香炉，恐不恰。可能是指四月的花香在六月骄阳之下燃烧净尽。

[74]since 一字含义模糊，第一至四行大意可能是:“不要因我永久赞美一人便以我为崇拜偶像”，亦可解为:“因为我是仅仅赞美一个人，所以不可指我为

崇拜偶像（意谓偶像崇拜者所崇拜的对象必不止一人)”。前一义似较胜。

[75]skill 一字，在四开本作 still，Tyrwhitt 改为 skill，近代本多从之。第十一至十四行的大意是:“古人未及见我的朋友之美貌，纵然笔下写得淋漓尽致，只是揣想，眼前没有模特儿；我们生逢现世，眼前看到模特儿，又苦无古人那样的生花妙笔给他写照。”

[76]“人间的明月”（The mortal moon）所度过的晦蚀，究何所指？Ingram & Redpath 列举不同的学说如下:

（一）西班牙无畏舰队，一五八八年（Butler, Hotson）

（二）女王六十三岁大关，一五九五—一五九六年（G.B. Harrison）

（三）女王政躬违和，一五九九—一六〇〇年（E.K. Chambers）

（四）哀塞克斯之叛变，一六〇一年（Thomas Tyler）

（五）女王之死，一六〇三年（Massey、Minto、Lee、Beeching）

（六）一次月蚀，例如一五九五年（O. F. Emerson）

（七）女王恩宠之消灭（Conrad）
一般相信，“明月”系指女王无疑，“晦蚀”何所指则无法确定。但这一点关系重大，因由此可以推定诗之著作年代也。endure 一字，是“安然度过”之意，不是“屈服于”或“受……之害”之意，故谓“女王之死”似不可能。

[77] 牛津本及一般近代本均从四开本的标点，不甚妥，兹从最近版本略加改动，语气较顺。

[78] 从一〇九至一二六首为一段落，主题是回顾友谊之经过，如何遭遇风波，如何重归于好。

[79] 前二行可能是指莎士比亚之以演员为业，时常在剧院与贵族之家演出，但亦可能是象征的写法，言其交游广阔，到处结识新交而又不能始终如一，成为大众取笑之对象。

[80] 第四行一般解释为“结新交而忘旧友”。Ingram & Redpath 注云:“Made each new attachment into yet another instance of the old offence of infidelity.”，似较佳。

[81] 第七、八两行费解。大意似应是如 Ingram & Redpath 所说:“There being no one else who exists for me and for whom I exist in such a way that they can change my hardened

sensibility either for good or for evil."。第八行字句顺序应为: That changes my steeled sense or（either）right or wrong。

[82] adder's sense 指传说中蛇以一耳着地，以尾端塞另一耳，拒抗捕蛇者之乐声咒语。

[83] 第十四行四开本作: That all the world besides me thinkes y'are dead。近代本有不同的修改，牛津本是遵从 Capell 的与 Steevens 的揣测，改为: That all the world besides methinks are dead。今照译。

[84] part 一字 Malone 提议作副词解，后 Beeching、Tucker 从之，最近威尔孙亦采用其说，认定 part = partly。意谓眼之机能有二，一是看，二是把看到的印象送到心里。诗人心里充满了他的爱友，不可能再吸收别的印象，眼有所见亦均幻作爱友之姿态，故眼只能执行前一机能，无法执行后一机能，所以总是部分地瞎了。

[85] 四开本作: My most true mind thus maketh mine untrue，牛津本从之。但有若干近代本改作 maketh mine eye untrue。如承认 untrue = untruth，则改动似不必要，因所谓 untruth 即是指眼睛之迷离恍惚误以一切形状皆为爱友之姿态也。

[86] 旧日观念以为眼睛确实射出光芒，在光芒照耀之下故能看到事物。

[87] 四开本第十四行末的标点是一个句点，后来有人改为问号，意义相差甚多，牛津本亦作问号，最近编本则多已改回四开本原状。第十三及十四行是回答第十行 Might I not then say ‘Now I love you best’（say so = say that “Now I love you best”）。

[88] 这是最著名的一首。“此诗既非吁请他的朋友对他忠实，亦非为诗人自己行为辩护，更不是解释朋友对他的猜疑，而只是企图为理想的爱情做一定义。”（Ingram & Redpath）Tucker Brooke 指出此诗用字百分之七十五是单音字，只有三个字音节在两个以上，没有一个字可以算是属于“诗的辞藻”。诗中无奥义，无怪诞玄妙的思想。韵法也平正调和。全诗一百一十个字，结构简单明了，洵杰作也。

[89] alteration 可能指变心（infidelity），但更可能指一般情形（circumstance），或如 Ingram & Redpath 所谓“指无情岁月使容颜发生之变化”。

[90] “Or inclines to withdraw when the other party's love withdraws.”（Ingram & Redpath）

[91] 星指北极星，据星相学星对人事万物具有奥秘之影响力，不可究诘，但对航海者有实用价值，测其高

度即可获知方向也。

[92] 等于是说意乱情迷之际瞎了眼睛。但是“诗人在此也许是暗示他当时眷恋的一些女人乃是比他地位较低之人（犹如在较低贱轨迹中游行之众星），同时另一含义则是只有他的爱友才是与他地位相埒也。”（Ingram & Redpath）此说亦不无见地。

[93] Ingram & Redpath 的释义可资参考: “The fact that you were once unkind to me serves me a friendly turn ; for，otherwise，when I recall the anguish that I then felt，I should be quite beaten down under the sense of the wrong I have done you，unless my fibre were as tough as brass or hammered steel. For if you have been shaken by my unkindness as I was then by yours，you have gone through a hellish time ; and I，tyrant-like，have given no leisure to considering how I once suffered from your offence to me（and so how you must now have suffered from mine）. Would that time of anguish we then suffered might have put me in mind in my deepest feelings how sharply real sorrow hurts，and

so might indirectly（through impelling me to act）have offered to you now，with the same promptness as you then did to me，the salve of apology and humility which is apt for wounded hearts! But the wrong you did me then now becomes the ransom money for my offence ; for my injury to you expiates yours to me，and you must in turn allow yours to expiate mine.”。

[94] 第三行的 so 是指第一行的 vile 而言。

[95]pyramids 可能泛指一般大建筑物；但亦可能特指一五八五至一五九〇年间罗马教皇 Sixtus 五世所掘出并且改建或修饰的方锥塔 obelisks ；亦可能指一六〇四年三月十五日英王哲姆斯正式进入伦敦时街道上所建之方锥塔（此种塔为欢迎布置之一部分，据云高六十英尺，内部有灯光设备）。

[96] 这一首难解。无疑地里面有我们所不明了的典实，但如威尔孙之依据 Beeching 将全首解释成为与当时政治有关的暗喻，则似无此必要。全诗大意仍是一贯的诗人自诉其情意之真挚，不因环境改变而生异心。

[97] 最后两行意义不明显。Ingram & Redpath 的

释义是：“I cite in support of this the cases of those utter time-servers who，after a life of wrong-doing，renounce their time-serving to die for perminent values.”。所谓 the fools of Time 究何所指？历来注者意见不一，或谓为 Jesuit conspirators，或谓指 Gunpowder Plot，或以为是 Essex and his followers，或猜是 Foxe's Martyrs，均属臆测，无可佐证。不论隐指何人何事，字面的意义想应是：“我的热情永恒不变，那些随波逐流一生为恶终于皈善的势利小人可为我证明也。”

[98] 第十三行所谓攻讦者（informer）指控诗人对其爱友故作忠贞之状而实则希图附骥名垂不朽，诗人斥其诬妄，全诗关键在第九行之“心”字，盖诗人之爱不拘形迹也。攻讦之人为谁，可不必究。

[99] 华盖（canopy），是帝王或显贵出巡时由亲信在其头上擎举之伞状仪仗。

[100] 此诗共十二行，每两行叶韵。伊利沙白时代之十四行诗，常有行数与韵法发生不规则之情事。此诗四开本于第十三、十四两行处留空白加括弧，表示此诗乃未完成之作品。实则此诗系一首完整作品，没有再加两行之可能。全集至第一二六首为一大段落，故

此诗显系 envoy（煞尾）性质，体裁亦特异也。

[101] 自一二七至一五二首为一组，这是大家公认的，但是这一组内各诗之次序应如何安排则迄无定论。这一组的主要对象是“黑女郎”（the Dark Lady）。据 Campbell 的分析:

127—132 Enter the Dark Lady

133—142 The Dark Lady

143—152 Exit the Dark Lady

[102] 四开本第九行是 my Mistress eyes，第十行是 Her eyes，语意完全重复，显有误植，近代本有几种不同的改动，牛津本遵 the Globe editors 作“my mistress’ brows...Her eyes”，今照译。

[103] 第五行 jacks 一字，似是莎士比亚误用音乐名词之一例。据 Onions 的解释，jacks 为“In the virginal，an upright piece of wood fixed to the key-lever and fitted with a quill which plucked the strings as the jack rose when the key was pressed down. Here used as ‘key’.”。上述解释之最后一句正是为莎士比亚做解说。按 virginal 为十六世纪通行之乐器，是近代钢琴之前驱，为少女所喜爱演奏，故名，长方箱型，可置案头亦可置怀中。所谓 jacks 不是手按之木键盘，而是在箱内

竖立之木键，不可能跳起触及演奏者之手掌。E.W. Naylor 的解释："The lady，having removed the rail which ordinarily stops the 'jacks' from jumping right out of the instrument when the keys are struck，was leaning over her work，testing it by striking the defective note，and holding the 'tender inward' of her hand over the 'jack' to prevent it from flying to the order end of the room."，似嫌牵强。

[104] 这是著名的一首，主题是 lust，诗里表现出对于性交之强烈的厌恶。有些人特别推崇这一首，例如 Bernard Shaw 说此诗乃英文学中之"the most merciless passage"，又如 Theodore Watts Duncan 认为此诗乃"the greatest sonnet in the world"，似嫌过分夸张其词。（可参看 Hilton Landry：*Interpretations in Shakespeare，Sonnets*，pp.96—104）

[105] 此诗主旨在最后两行。诗人排斥传统的写法，不欲将其爱人之美妄加比拟，然并非不承认其美也。威尔孙指出，此诗常被误解，例如 Brandes 说："莎士比亚明白说过……这女人没有美貌。"萧伯纳也有同样误解。Jordan 于一八八一年就主张说过莎士比

亚如此贬抑的女人必是一个黑人!

[106] 在这一首诗里，诗人、朋友、情妇又以三角恋爱的关系出现，但是这首诗是诗人首次直接向情妇呼吁。

[107] 原文 bail 一字，诚如 Ingram & Redpath 所说，不是“保释出狱（bail out of prison）”之意，应解作 confine（牛津大字典 OED.V3.1 即引此句为例句）。故译作“包起”，兼寓保护之意。意谓：你把我关在你的心里，我愿把我的朋友再关在我的心里，一层套着一层地包起来。

[108] guard = guard-house，监牢。

[109] T. G. Tucker，注释最后两行曰:“In imprisoning me，you are imprisoning all that is in me，and he is in my heart ; therefore whatever harshness you show to me affects him also，and I shall feel for him any rigour which I should not feel for myself.”。

[110] Tucker 注云:“这女人强迫两个男人困惑于她的美貌而同时对她缱绻。她坚持享有诗人及其朋友，因诗人不能满足其欲望。他戏作请求，谓其友仅是他的替身，他愿独任其劳，如她肯放他的朋友。但该女人及其朋友均无此意向。”

[111] 一三五和一三六两首都是玩弄 Will 一字之双关义：一方面是一个人的名字，他可能是诗人自己，可能是他的朋友，可能是女人的丈夫。另一方面 Will = desire ; volition。但是 Ingram & Redpath 注: “there is，quite apart from personal name allusions，the common cant sense of the *membrum pudendum*，male or female. Most commentators seem to have been innocent or reticent in respect of this meaning....”，颇值得注意。

[112] Tyler 对第十一、十二两行注: Make me of no account，if you will，but still love me，regard me as “a something sweet to thee.”。

[113] 此诗初见于一五九九年初版之 *The Passionate Pilgrim*，其中颇多异文，显然是此诗之初稿，如下:

When my love swears that she is made of truth,
I do believe her，though I know she lies,
That she might think me some untutored youth,
Unskilful in the world's false *forgeries.*

Thus vainly thinking that she thinks me young,
Although *I know* my *years be* past the best,
I *smiling* credit her false-speaking tongue,
Outfacing faults in love with love's ill rest.
But wherefore says *my love that she is young*？
And wherefore say not I that I am old？
O，love's best habit is *a soothing tongue*，
And age，in love，loves not to have years told.
Therefore *I'll lie with love*，and *love* with me,
Since that our faults in love thus smothered be.

诗中的斜体字句是见于初稿中之异文，看看本诗如何修改初稿，那是很有兴味的事。

[114] 对情妇之冷漠无情曲加谅解，乃是十四行诗之传统题材的一部分。

[115] 所谓五种心智（five wits）即common wit、imagination、fantasy、estimation，and memory。为五种感官之对。

[116] 关于最后两行Ingram & Redpath引述Samuel Butler的释文："I shall suffer less for my sin hereafter，for I get some of the

punishment coincidently with the offence."。言犯奸时已受相当惩罚，此后受苦可以较少也。

[117] 此诗曾见于 *The Passionate Pilgrim*，1599，其文字略有出入，如下:

Two loues I haue，of Comfort and Despaire,
That like two Spirits，do suggest me still：
My better Angell，is a Man（right faire）
My worser spirite a Woman（colour'd ill.）
To win me soone to hell，my Female euill
Tempteth my better Angell from my side：
And would corrupt my Saint to be a Diuell,
Wooing his puritie with her faire pride.
And whether that my Angell be turnde feend,
Suspect I may（yet not directly tell：）
For being both to me：both，to each friend,
I ghesse one Angell in anothers hell：
　　The truth I shall not know，but liue in dout,
　　Till my bad Angell fire my good one out.

与四开本主要不同之点为:（一）第二行之 that 四开本作 which；（二）第三行及第四行之 my 四开本作 the；（三）第六行之 side 四开本作 sight；（四）

第八行之 faire 四开本作 fowle；（五）第九行之 feend 四开本作 fine；（六）第十一行之 For being both to 四开本作 But being both from me；（七）第十三行之 The truth I shall not 四开本作 Yet this shall I ne' er。其中第三点及第五点均优于四开本，近代本多从之。

[118] comfort and despair = salvation and damnation。

[119] 所谓 hell，系引用 Boccaccio 之关于 Rustico and Alibech 的故事（见 *Decameron*，Ⅲ，10），= female sexual organ。

[120] fire out = infect with a venereal disease（Ingram & Redpath）。

[121] 此诗内容俗浅，体裁亦异，采用较短之诗行，每行八个音节，不合十四行诗之惯例，故有人疑非出自莎氏手笔，至少此诗是与集中其他诸作大不相侔。

[122] 四开本第二行原文是: My sinful earth these rebel powers that thee array，这一行前三个字与第一行末后三个字重复，而且有十二个音节，显然是手民之误，但是删去这三个字之后应该填补怎样的两个音节，却莫衷一是。Ingram & Redpath（pp.358—359）胪列了九十九个不同的提议，那

还只是一部分。牛津本遵从 Malone 的建议，采用 Fool'd by。

[123] 第一、第二两行中之 conscience，有双关义：（一）良心;（二）通奸。诗中其他数字，如 rising、rise、stand、fall 皆有猥亵的双关义，不需详细解说。

[124] misuse = misrepresent（做不真实的陈述）。

[125] 四开本作 more perjured eye，后 Sewell（1725）改 eye 为 I，近代本多从之。

[126] 最后两首诗性质很特殊。内容相同，写法稍异，与集中其他各诗全无关联，且其内容所云，显然翻译性质。其来源不易确定，因其内容乃过去诗歌中所常见者，最早的是五世纪时 Byzantine Marianus Scholasticus 所作一首短诗 epigram（Ⅸ.627, *the Palatine Anthology*），厥后直到十六世纪陆续有拉丁文、意大利文、法文的写作。我们很难断定莎士比亚所采用的蓝本是哪一个。有人且疑这两首诗非出自莎氏手笔。

著作权合同登记号：字18-2024-251

图书在版编目（CIP）数据

莎士比亚十四行诗 : 汉文、英文 / (英) 威廉 · 莎士比亚著 ; 梁实秋译 . -- 长沙 : 湖南文艺出版社 , 2025. 7. -- ISBN 978-7-5726-2507-7

Ⅰ . I561.23

中国国家版本馆 CIP 数据核字第 20258WH718 号

上架建议：畅销 · 文学

SHASHIBIYA SHISIHANGSHI: HANWEN、YINGWEN

莎士比亚十四行诗：汉文、英文

著　　者：［英］威廉 · 莎士比亚
译　　者：梁实秋
出 版 人：陈新文
责任编辑：熊宇亮
监　　制：秦　青　毛闽峰
图书策划：王心悦　史义伟
营销编辑：柯慧萍　刘　珣　李春雪
版权支持：王媛媛　辛　艳
装帧设计：利　锐
出　　版：湖南文艺出版社
（长沙市雨花区东二环一段 508 号　邮编：410014）
网　　址：www.hnwy.net
印　　刷：北京中科印刷有限公司
开　　本：760 mm × 960 mm　1/32
字　　数：228 千字
印　　张：12
版　　次：2025 年 7 月第 1 版
印　　次：2025 年 7 月第 1 次印刷
书　　号：ISBN 978-7-5726-2507-7
定　　价：59.80 元

若有质量问题，请致电质量监督电话：010-59096394
团购电话：010-59320018